# Falling for a
# COWBOY'S
# SMILE

## A TENDER HEART TEXAS NOVEL

# KATIE LANE

*To my Jimmy,*
*Here's to 40 more years of love, laughter, and arguing*
*over who's right . . . deep down, you know that I am*

*"Daisy McNeil hadn't come out west to be someone's bride. She'd come out west for adventure. And she intended to find some."*
  –Tender Heart, Book Nine

# CHAPTER ONE

❧

NOTHING HAD CHANGED IN BLISS, Texas. Gracie Lynn Arrington took comfort in that.

Emmett Daily, who ran the only gas station in town, sat at a table arguing and playing dominos with Old Man Sims. Emmett's wife, Joanna, hustled around serving cake to the guests and making sure the DJ knew what songs to play. Ms. Marble, a retired schoolteacher and the baker of the beautiful wedding cake, was getting after some teenagers for racing through the reception tent with sparklers. Mrs. Crawley was gossiping with a group of townswomen, her mouth going a mile a minute. Most of the people Gracie's age were out on the dance floor, kicking up their heels.

Gracie would've loved to join them, but it was a little hard to kick up your heels when you couldn't take a step without your walker.

"You want to give it a shot, Brat?"

She turned to find her half-brother Cole standing there looking as tall, dark, and handsome as ever in his white tux shirt and black pants. He was the spitting image of his daddy, while Gracie looked just like their mama.

"I think I'll pass," she said. "I'm stuffed after eating two slices of Ms. Marble's wedding cake. I couldn't decide on chocolate or strawberry. So I had both."

"Why, you little piglet." Cole reached out to ruffle her hair, something he'd done ever since she could remember, but then hesitated. "Emery says I need to stop doing that. She says women hate having their hair messed." He glanced around and smiled slyly. "But since she's not here to get after me . . . " He messed her hair.

Gracie laughed and slapped at his hand. "Where is Emery, anyway?"

He rolled his eyes. "Where else? She's at Aunt Lucy's gravesite."

Cole's great-aunt Lucy Arrington had been the author of the classic Tender Heart series. It was a set of ten novels based on the mail-order brides who came to Bliss, Texas, in the late 1800s to wed the cowboys who worked the huge Arrington ranch. Lucy had died before writing the eleventh book in the series . . . or so everyone had thought until Gracie stumbled upon a chapter in the little white chapel. That night had changed her life forever.

And not in a good way.

She smiled and tried not to show the fear that always accompanied any reminder of the accident. "She loves Lucy. She's probably just showing her respect."

"Or looking for the rest of the chapter." He waved at Emmett. Cole worked as a mechanic at the gas station, but he didn't want to fix cars for a living. He wanted to breed horses. But in order to build his horse ranch, he needed money, something that had always been scarce in their family.

Gracie perked up. "The rest of what chapter?"

He turned to her, and his cheeks flushed a rosy pink. Blushing was the one physical trait he and Gracie had in common. They blushed when they were embarrassed or lying . . . or when they said something they shouldn't have said.

Her heart rate picked up, and she squeezed Cole's arm in excitement. "Emery found another chapter while I was gone, didn't she? She was right. Lucy didn't just finish one chapter."

Cole glanced around before he shushed her. "Would you keep it down? Most of the town has been looking for that book since you found the first chapter. If word gets out we found another, there will be complete mayhem. Besides, Emery didn't find another chapter in the cemetery. She only found one page."

"But if she found one page, there has to be more." She went to reach for the walker that stood next to her chair, but Cole stopped her.

"This was exactly why I didn't mention finding the page. You don't think clearly when it comes to that book."

"But if we can find all the chapters, it will solve everything, Cole. With your share of the royalties, you can pay off my hospital bills and build new stables for your horse ranch—"

He held up a hand. "Stop living in a fantasy world, Gracie. That book has been missing for fifty years and only one chapter and a page have been found. If Lucy finished the book—and that's a big if—the other chapters might not turn up for another fifty years. Which is why I'm thinking you should just sell the chapter that you found and be done with it."

Her eyes widened. "I could never do that, Cole. Lucy wanted that book published as a complete novel. I know in my heart that she did."

"You sound like Emery." He paused. "Although since we've been married she hasn't brought up the book much at all."

Gracie understood why. It was hard to discuss Tender Heart with a non-believer. And as much as she loved her brother, he was a non-believer. Tender Heart was just a fictional series to him, written by a selfish woman who hadn't left a dime of her royalties to her family. But Lucy had left the final book for the Arringtons to find. Gracie was sure of it.

Something over her shoulder caught Cole's attention, and she didn't have to turn around to know who it was. His eyes filled with happiness and unconditional love. "I'll talk to you later, Brat," he said. Gracie watched as he moved around the tables to the tent opening where Emery stood. He pulled her into his arms as if he couldn't wait to touch her.

The sight made Gracie happy and a little envious. What would it be like to have a man love you like that? Her gaze swept over the wedding guests, but the cowboy she searched for was nowhere in sight.

"Catch!"

The loudly spoken word caused her to swivel in her chair. Her cousin and best friend Becky stood there, looking a little worse for wear. Her golden brown hair was falling out of its up-do and her mascara was smudged beneath her dark Arrington blue eyes. Eyes that twinkled with mischief as she drew back her arm and threw her bouquet like a slow-pitch softball. The flowers hit Gracie right in the chest before she caught them, sending pink rose petals to her lap.

She laughed. "What are you doing?"

Becky slipped into the chair next to her. "What does it look like I'm doing? I just tossed my bouquet."

Gracie rolled her eyes. "You can't toss it to only one person, Beck. You have to give all the single ladies a chance to catch it." She went to hand the bouquet back, but Becky refused to take it.

"I'm not tossing it for Winnie Crawley to catch. I couldn't live with myself if I helped saddle some poor guy with that woman." She smiled. "Besides, I want my favorite cousin to be next in line for a wedding."

Gracie set the bouquet on the table. "I don't think that's going to happen. Few men want to be stuck with a crip—"

Becky cut her off. "Don't you dare say it, Gracie Lynn. Not when you just got through walking down the aisle without one stumble."

"Only because I had a walker to hang on to."

Becky's chin turned stubborn. "Two months ago,

you were in a wheelchair. I'd say that walking with a walker is a pretty big accomplishment. And in another month, I have no doubt that we'll toss the walker like I did my bouquet."

That's what her physical therapists at the Dallas rehabilitation center, where she'd spent the last few months, believed. In fact, they believed that she should already be walking on her own. But not one of her therapists had ever been thrown from a horse. Or woken up in a hospital unable to move their legs. Or spent months in a wheelchair. They didn't understand the trauma her body had been through.

Gracie needed the walker. Her legs were still too shaky and undependable. And she worried that they always would be. But before she voiced her fears, Becky's brand-new husband walked up.

Mason Granger was as tall, dark, and handsome as Cole, but a lot more serious. Gracie couldn't help but wonder how her vivacious cousin had fallen for such a stoic man who liked to give orders.

He held out a hand. "Dance with me."

Becky ignored his hand and sent him a sassy look. "I think you forgot the magic word."

Mason cocked an eyebrow, then smiled brighter than Gracie had ever seen him smile. "Please, Mrs. Granger."

The sassy look turned to one of adoration as Becky took his hand and allowed him to pull her to her feet. She gave him a brief kiss before she turned to Gracie. "Come on and dance with—"

A loud rumble cut her off, and all three of them glanced up. Another rolling rumble had the music stopping and the guests freezing in place as they looked up at the tent ceiling and waited. They didn't have long to wait. The next peal of thunder was followed by the splatter of raindrops on canvas.

"Yee-haws" filled the tent as the entire crowd moved as one to the opening. It had been a hot, dry summer. They badly needed the rain.

It took Gracie a while to follow. She had been sitting for too long and her leg muscles had tightened up. Terrified that she would fall, she went slowly. By the time she made it outside, the rain was coming down harder, and the entire town was dancing around in celebration.

She stood in the shelter of the tent and watched with a full heart. She'd missed her family and the people of Bliss more then she could ever put into words when she'd been at the rehabilitation center for over two months. This was the only home she'd ever known. The only place she ever wanted to live.

"Baby Girl!" Becky's brother and Gracie's cousin Zane came out of the crowd and scooped her up into his arms like she was a toddler, splattering her dress with the rain that dripped from his cowboy hat. Of course, a second later she had more than drips on her when he stepped out in the rain and spun her around. Then he passed her to Cole, who took a turn spinning her before passing her to another person who passed her to another. By the time she was set on her feet, she was soaked to the skin and completely out of breath from laughing.

She stood there for a few moments enjoying the celebration until she realized she didn't have her walker. She glanced around and found it sitting by the opening of the tent, a good ten feet away.

Panic gripped her. She had walked more than ten feet without her walker at the rehabilitation center, but never without parallel bars to grab onto. Nor had she done it in a soaking wet maid of honor's dress that suddenly felt like it weighed a hundred pounds.

But she didn't have much choice.

The heels of her pink cowboy boots had sunk into the wet ground, and it took all her concentration to lift one foot. After only five steps, her muscles trembled like leaves in a strong wind, but she wasn't sure if that was from her fear of falling or the stress of walking. Fortunately, she didn't have that much farther to go. She bit her lip and took another step. Then another. But this time, the toe of her boot came down on the hem of her wet dress. The slight tug was all that was needed to send her sprawling to her hands and knees.

Humiliation welled up like the mud through her fingers. But before she could glance around to see who was watching, strong arms lifted her off the ground and cradled her against a hard chest. Her wet hair covered her face, but she didn't need to see to know who held her. Her body had grown a sensitivity to only one man.

"I got you, Miss Gracie."

The words spoken in the familiar deep East Texas twang had her heart thumping overtime and her cheeks burning in mortification. She wanted to hide behind her hair forever, but she finally pushed it out of her face and looked at the man who held her.

Dirk Hadley had gotten even more handsome while she'd been away. He looked taller. His shoulders seemed wider. And the biceps that flexed beneath his wet, transparent tuxedo shirt appeared even bigger. The Texas summer sun had lightened his hair to golden honey and toasted his skin to a rich brown. The tan made his grayish-blue eyes look even grayer and his smile even whiter. He flashed that smile. And just like that, Gracie forgot to breathe.

"You okay, Miss Gracie?" he asked. "You need me to call for Cole? Or maybe the doc?"

She looked away from those mind-altering eyes and shook her head. "I'm more embarrassed than hurt." She noticed the mud she was getting on his white shirt and lifted her hand from his chest. "I'm getting you all dirty."

His arms tightened. "A little dirt never hurt anyone. And as for embarrassed, there's no reason to be. All these yahoos are too busy celebrating to notice you taking a little spill."

But Dirk had noticed, the one person she didn't want to see her wallowing around in the mud like a dressed-up sow. Another roll of thunder rumbled through the skies, and the rain turned into a downpour.

"We better get you out of this," Dirk said.

He carried her around the celebrating townsfolk to the little white chapel where Becky and Mason had just gotten married. It had been built in the late 1800s so the mail-order brides would have a respectable place to wed their cowboys. And for one brief moment, Gracie pretended that she was one of those brides. Not an original bride, but her favorite fictional Tender Heart bride Daisy McNeil. While Gracie was nothing like feisty Daisy, it wasn't a stretch to imagine Dirk as the charming Tender Heart hero Johnny Earhart.

As Dirk hurried to the chapel, he bent his head so the brim of his cowboy hat shielded her head from the rain. With his face so close, she could see the darker bursts of deep blue in his gray irises and feel the heat of his beer-scented breath on her lips.

Suddenly, she felt lightheaded and woozy, as if she'd downed an entire six-pack of beer instead of two glasses of non-alcoholic punch. And when he shifted her to open the door, her arms tightened around his neck, her fingers brushing the heated skin beneath the damp collar of his shirt. The contrast of her cold skin to his hot had him pausing and glancing down at her.

The smart thing to do would be to remove her hand and look away as if nothing had happened. Unfortunately, her mind was too immersed in her Tender Heart fantasy to be smart. It prompted her to do something stupid.

Something very, very stupid.

*"Most folks in Tender Heart, Texas, knew that God had given different gifts to the Earhart brothers. Rory got the brains, Duke got the brawn, and Johnny got the ability to charm the pantaloons off any woman."*

# CHAPTER TWO

❦

THE KISS COMPLETELY BLINDSIDED DIRK. He knew Gracie had a crush on him. It was hard not to notice the adoration in her beautiful turquoise blue eyes whenever she looked at him. He just never thought she'd be bold enough to kiss him. That just wasn't Gracie. She was kind, shy, and unassuming—the type of girl who gives rather than takes.

But she was taking now. Her warm, sweet mouth was taking all the brain cells right out of his head and all the willpower right out of his body. And he wanted nothing more than to deepen the kiss and do a little taking of his own. But he couldn't let that happen. He liked Gracie too much.

He pulled back from the kiss and said the first thing that popped into his head. "Well, thank you, Miss Gracie. That was real nice." He mentally cringed, but kept a smile on his face as her cheeks turned a bright pink. After the stupid comment, he felt a little embarrassed himself.

He quickly carried her over to a pew and set her down. Since meeting her, he'd worked real hard to ignore the nice set of breasts she'd been blessed with. But it was hard to ignore them when her pink dress had turned to tissue paper and he could see the sweet swell of her cleavage spilling over her lacy bra. He cleared his throat and looked away.

"Why don't you rest here while I go get Cole to take you home?" he said.

"No!" When he glanced back, her cheeks flamed brighter and she lowered her gaze to her lap. "I didn't mean to yell. It's just that Cole has been working so hard lately, I don't want to ruin his one night out with Emery. All I need is to rest my legs for a while." She lifted her gaze. "If you bring me my walker, you can go back to the party. I'll be fine by myself."

He wanted to take her up on it. His lips still tingled from the kiss, and his eyes kept straying to her breasts. He could use some fresh air . . . and maybe a stiff shot of tequila. But he couldn't bring himself to leave her.

He took off his hat. "I could use a little break myself." He moved into the pew in front of hers and sat down. The pink netting that adorned the end of the pews got stuck on his boot heel. He crossed his foot onto his knee to pluck it off.

"I didn't take Becky for a pink fluff kind of gal. I expected the chapel to be decorated in denim and rope."

Gracie laughed. She had a nice laugh. It wasn't loud or forced like some women's. Instead, it trickled out all soft and natural like wind through chimes. It helped ease his discomfort, and he turned to her.

"Come on now. You know Becky better than anyone. She's more tough denim than girlie pink." He rested his arm along the back of the pew and grinned. "Now you, on the other hand, are girlie and pink." He meant it as a compliment, but it didn't look like she took it that way. Her smile faded, and her brow knitted.

"You're right. Becky is a lot tougher than I am. She probably would've chosen denim and rope if her mama hadn't been so set on a pink wedding. It was Lucy Arrington's favorite color."

The name never failed to annoy Dirk. And with a couple beers in his system, a little of that annoyance leaked out. "It seems that no matter what happens in this town it always comes back to Lucy Arrington. Why is that? It's not like she was the one who started Bliss. She didn't ranch, or strike oil, or build anything. She was just an eccentric old maid who lived in a fantasy world."

Gracie bristled up like a cat when a stray dog wandered too close. "How can you say that? She immortalized this town with her writing."

He should've let it go. But he didn't. Maybe because his mind was still filled with thoughts of her warm lips and an argument was the perfect distraction. Or maybe because he was getting sick of going along with the town's infatuation with Lucy.

"From what I can tell," he said, "Lucy exploited this town and her family, then died, leaving nothing to Bliss or the Arringtons . . . except a few measly chapters of the final book."

Dirk didn't realize what he'd said until Gracie's eyes widened. Her voice was hushed and excited. "A few?"

He pulled his hat on and got to his feet. "I think we're all rested up. If you tell me where your walker is, I'll go get it."

She grabbed the pew in front of her and stood. He had to admit that he was damned proud of the progress she'd made at the rehab center. He also had to admit that it was easier to ignore her pretty turquoise eyes when she was sitting and much harder when she was standing.

She had looked so petite and fragile sitting in her wheelchair, but she didn't look fragile now. She was taller than he'd thought. He was six foot one, and she was no more than five inches shorter. She was slender, but not skinny. Her arms were toned and defined, no doubt from spending months pushing around her wheelchair.

"Don't you dare lie to me, Dirk Hadley," she said. "Other chapters have been found, haven't they?" Her voice grew even more excited. "How many? And who found—"

The chapel door flew open, and Cole charged in looking wet and scared. His face registered relief when he saw Gracie. "Are you okay? When I found your walker I got worried something had happened to you."

Before Gracie could reply, Zane came striding in. His tux shirt was soaked and rain dripped from his cowboy hat. "Cole, I looked in the cemetery, but I didn't—" He cut off when he saw Gracie. "Damn, Baby Girl, you scared the hell out of us. The entire town is looking for you."

"That's my fault," Dirk cut in. "I should've let Cole know that I had brought Gracie here to get her out of the rain. We got to talking and lost track of the time."

Both men turned to him, but their reactions were completely different. Zane smiled knowingly while Cole's gaze narrowed dangerously. Dirk was a little confused until Zane spoke.

"That's sure a pretty shade of pink lipstick you're wearin', Dirk."

Well, shit. This wasn't going to turn out well.

Before Dirk could think of some way to defuse the situation and not get beaten half to death by Cole, Gracie spoke up. "I kissed him."

When all three men turned to her, she merely blushed and shrugged her shoulders. "I guess I had too much champagne."

Zane released the tension in the room by laughing and winking at Gracie. "It looks like you handle liquor like the rest of the Arringtons." He walked over and swept her up in his arms. "Come on, Baby Girl, let's go find you something less intoxicating to drink." He headed for the door.

Dirk started to follow, but Cole stopped him with a firm grip on his arm. He waited for the door to close behind Zane and Gracie before he spoke. "I think we both know she was lying. Gracie can't have alcohol with the muscle relaxers she needs to take at night."

Dirk held up his hands. "I give you my word that I didn't take advantage of her, Cole. I would never do that to Gracie."

Cole released his arm. "I know." He ran a hand through his wet hair and stared at one of the stained-glass windows that lined the walls of the chapel. "She thinks she's in love with you."

Even though Dirk knew how Gracie felt, it was damned hard hearing it put into words. He almost wished Cole had just punched him. "She doesn't love me," he said. "It's just a crush."

Cole looked at him. "I know. But why do you think they call them that? Gracie is going to be crushed when it finally sinks in that you don't return her affections." His eyes narrowed. "You don't, do you?"

It was a tough question. He couldn't deny that he cared about Gracie. They had gotten close when he'd worked on the Arrington Ranch. And if he had plans to stay in Bliss, he might've let those feelings turn into something more than friendship. But he wasn't staying. He couldn't.

He slowly shook his head.

"That's what I thought." Cole paused. "I think it's best if you stay away from my sister."

"It's a little hard to stay away from people in a town the size of Bliss."

Cole placed his hands on his hips and stared down at his muddy boots. "When you first came to town, I didn't like you much. You were too cocky and too much of a damn know-it-all." He lifted his eyes. "It took me a while to figure out that beneath all that cockiness was a hardworking, honest man who anyone would be proud to call a friend."

Yep, Dirk wished Cole had just beaten the hell out of him and been done with it. Instead, he was beating him up with guilt. Dirk wasn't honest. And he sure as hell wasn't a good friend.

"But despite our friendship," Cole continued,

"my family will always come first. Gracie has been through enough in the last year. She doesn't need to get her heart broken on top of everything else. Which is why it's time for you to move on."

Dirk couldn't argue the point. It *was* time he moved on. It was past time. He'd been in Bliss much longer than he'd intended. Unfortunately, Cole was right. Family did come first. That's why he couldn't leave. Not until he knew the truth. He was getting closer to it everyday. All he needed was a few more weeks. A month tops.

"I can't leave yet," he said. "I promised Carly I'd run the diner for her while she goes to Atlanta for Savannah's wedding. But I promise I'll head out soon. And until then, I'll steer clear of Gracie."

That seemed to satisfy Cole. He nodded before he pushed Dirk toward the door. "Come on, I'll buy you a beer."

☾

The people of Bliss partied as hard as they worked. It was close to one o'clock in the morning by the time Dirk hitched a ride with Winnie Crawley back to town. Or not hitched as much as drove. Winnie was drunker than Cooter Brown, and when he saw her stumbling to her car, he couldn't let her drive. Especially since it was raining cats and dogs.

He regretted the decision as soon as they were on the highway. Winnie was sexually aggressive when she was sober. Drunk, she was like a dog in heat. He thought the console would keep her in her seat, but Winnie straddled it like a world-class bull rider and proceeded to maul the hell out of him.

"I knew you was-s-s after me, Dirk Hadley." She furrowed her long fingernails through his hair while her other hand ran along the inseam of his pants.

He grabbed it before she could sink her claws into his package. "Now settle down, Winnie. I'm not after you. I'm just driving you home."

She nibbled on his ear, and damned if chills didn't run down his spine. And not the good kind. "I can't go home. My daddy will tan my hide if I come home drunk again." She kissed her way down his neck. "I guess I'll just have to sleep it off in your room at the motor lodge."

He pulled away. "Oh, no, you're not. I just got back in your mama's good graces. I'm not getting kicked out of the motor lodge again."

She continued to nibble on his neck. "She couldn't kick you out if you became her son-in-law."

The thought of being married to Winnie gave him more than chills. It made him a little sick to his stomach. "Now, honey, why would you want to marry a good-for-nothing drifter like—shit!" He pushed her away and grabbed his neck. "Did you just give me a hickey?"

She fell back in the passenger seat and smiled like a cat that got the cream. "Now you have a Winnie mark."

Dirk was so pissed he wanted to stop the car, get out, and let her drive herself home. Instead, he pushed down his anger and pressed harder on the accelerator. The quicker he got to town, the quicker he could get rid of her. But as soon as they passed the town limits, Winnie started squirming in her seat.

"I gotta pee."

"Hold it. We're almost to your house."

She pressed her hands between her legs. "I can't hold it. If you don't get me to a bathroom now, I'm gonna pee my pants." The frantic look in her eyes said she wasn't kidding.

Since the few businesses in town were closed up tight, he was forced to pull into the motor lodge. She jumped out of the car before he even came to a full stop. By the time he got to the door of his room, she was jumping around like she had fire ants in her pants.

"Hurry!"

He unlocked the door, and she raced inside to the bathroom. Just in case someone drove by and spotted her car, he decided it was best if he waited outside. But when a few minutes had passed and she still hadn't come out, he unlocked the door and peeked in. The narrow strip of light that spilled in from the open door was enough to see Winnie passed out on his bed. Her hair covered her face, the hem of her dress was stuck in her panties, and one high heel had dropped to the floor.

Dirk released an agitated sigh and stepped into the room. The door closed behind him, shrouding the room in darkness. He didn't stop to turn on a light. The quicker he got Winnie home, the better. He started to lean down and pick her up when the scent of cigarette smoke filled his nostrils. And since Winnie hadn't had time to light up, a prickle of apprehension tiptoed up Dirk's spine. He straightened and slowly turned. In the dark corner where the chair was, the orange tip of a lit cigarette glowed.

There was an inhalation of breath, and another puff of smoke billowed toward Dirk . . . followed by a familiar voice.

"I guess the old adage is true. Like daddy, like son."

*"As soon as she stepped off the stage, Daisy felt like a prize cow being auctioned off at the county fair. And since she had no intentions of being anyone's prize cow, she wasn't exactly polite. 'If you'd stop gawking and point me in the direction of the boardinghouse, I'd be much obliged.'"*

# Chapter Three

༄

"I CAN'T BELIEVE YOU DIDN'T TELL me about the other chapters that have been found." Gracie was so upset that she spoke a little louder than usual.

She quickly glanced around Lucy's Place Diner to make sure no one had heard. Everyone seemed too busy enjoying their Sunday morning breakfast and chatting about Mason and Becky's wedding to pay attention to her. Everyone but Old Man Sims. He sat at the counter and stared directly at Gracie. But he couldn't have heard her. Mr. Sims was as deaf as a stone.

"I'm sorry," Emery said. "But I worried that if you found out about the other chapters, you would quit your therapy and come home." Her green eyes filled with sympathy as she reached across the table for Gracie's hand. "I know how much finding the final book means to you."

If anyone knew how much it meant to Gracie, Emery did. She was the only one besides Becky who knew how far Gracie had gone to try and sell the final Tender Heart book. If Emery hadn't kept her secret, Gracie might have gone to jail instead of rehab—or at least had to deal with a law suit for plagiarism.

When Gracie had first found the chapter in the chapel, she had no intention of forging the rest of the book. She'd just been excited to stumble upon an unpublished chapter by her favorite author. She'd ridden at full gallop back to the ranch to tell Cole and her stepfather. But as fate would have it, Cole had been heading down the same road in his truck. When he'd almost hit her, her horse reared and threw her off. Gracie landed on a boulder, rupturing a disk in her spine.

Cole said she was conscious the entire time it took for the paramedics to get there, but she didn't remember a thing. All she remembered was waking up in the hospital to find Cole sitting by her bed, his eyes swollen and bloodshot from crying. She thought his tears were only for her, but she soon learned that her stepfather Hef Arrington had died of a heart attack only a day after the accident while trying to remove the rock Gracie had fallen on.

The next few months had been hell. She'd struggled to recover, and Cole had struggled to pay her medical bills and keep the creditors away. Confined to a wheelchair, she had felt useless to help her brother. When she and Becky had looked everywhere and hadn't found any more chapters, Becky

had come up with the idea of Gracie finishing
Lucy's book and selling it.

It seemed like the perfect solution to all their
financial troubles. It wasn't until she sent a letter
to Emery, who was a New York editor at the time,
that she started to have doubts about being able
to pull off the hoax. She enjoyed writing, but she
was nowhere near as good as Lucy. And using her
great-aunt's typewriter and old typing paper wasn't
going to be enough to fool a professional.

But when Emery arrived in Bliss searching for
the woman who had written her the letter, it was
too late for doubts. As Gracie feared, once Emery
read the book, she knew immediately that all but
the first chapter was fake. She could've told her
publishers about Gracie's plagiarism. Instead, she'd
put her job on the line by saying she didn't know
who was responsible for the fraud.

Things had worked out in the end. Emery had
quit her job and moved to Bliss to marry Cole. But
Gracie couldn't stop feeling guilty. Not only had
she wronged Lucy Arrington, but she'd also lied to
Cole. And she wouldn't be able to forgive herself
until she'd found all the chapters.

"Are you sure that the other chapters are Lucy's?"
she asked.

Emery nodded. "We haven't found them in
numerical order, but they are in Lucy's voice."

"And they were found in different places around
town? By who?"

"Me, for one." Carly slid into the booth next to
Emery. Carly was a close friend of Emery's and had
just recently married Zane and reopened the diner.
"I found the tenth chapter right under your butt

when I was renovating the diner. The envelope was stuck down in the base of the booth. It makes sense. This is the same booth Lucy used to sit in when she came to the diner to plot her books." She nodded at the half-eaten omelet on Gracie's plate. "You didn't like your omelet? If something's wrong with it, I can make you another one." Carly was an amazing chef who was very sensitive about her cooking.

"No, it's delicious. I'm just not very hungry." Gracie's gaze swept to the kitchen pass-through. Dirk was setting two plates with bacon and eggs on the stainless-steel counter. As he rang the bell to let the waitresses know that an order was up, he glanced over. She quickly looked away as her face flooded with heat.

How could she be so stupid? If Dirk hadn't known she liked him before, he certainly knew it now. Kissing him like a moonstruck idiot had been a dead giveaway. Just like his embarrassment over the kiss had been a dead giveaway that he didn't return her feelings.

"I had an epiphany the other night," Emery interrupted Gracie's thoughts. "I've been so busy authenticating the writing and the paper the chapters were written on that I didn't give any thought to the envelopes the pages came in. I sent them to an antique book dealer who does forensic and age dating on paper so he could pinpoint their age."

"But why?" Gracie asked. "Don't they have to be the same age as the paper Lucy wrote the books on?"

"Not necessarily. Carly and I have been talking and it seems unlikely that Lucy hid the chapters right before she died. Not only was she sick with cancer and couldn't get around, but also, if she had hidden them over fifty years ago at least one of the chapters would've turned up long before now. Especially when everyone was looking for the final book."

Gracie rested her arms on the table. "You think someone hid them after Lucy's death?"

"I'm thinking long after. There's no other way to explain why so many chapters are showing up now when they didn't show up earlier."

"But who would hide them? And why?"

"That's what Carly and I have been trying to figure out."

"What can I do to help?" She wasn't surprised when Carly and Emery exchanged looks. No one thought Gracie was capable of helping with anything. Carly's next words proved it.

"You don't need to help. The only thing you need to worry about is getting stronger." She pushed the omelet closer to Gracie. "Now eat or I'm going to get a complex."

Not wanting to hurt Carly's feelings, Gracie took another bite as the conversation moved to their friend's upcoming wedding.

"Savannah called me three times this morning," Carly said. "I swear that girl is the worst Bridezilla ever. Now she's worried that we're burned out on weddings and won't come to Atlanta for hers. I told her we'd be there on Friday to spend an entire week catering to her every whim."

Emery laughed. "She called me too, but I'd turned off my phone so it wouldn't disturb Cole. He was still sleeping when Gracie and I left. He's been working so hard lately. Last night was the first time he's relaxed in a long time." She took a sip of her coffee and sighed. "I wish he'd come to Atlanta with me. We never got to go on a honeymoon and it would be so good for him to have a week off with no worries."

Gracie couldn't agree more. If anyone deserved a vacation, it was her brother. "But why can't he go?" she asked. "I'm sure he could get someone to cover for him at Emmett's garage."

Emery glanced at her. "But you just got back from the rehab center. We couldn't leave you alone."

It was hard to keep the annoyance from her voice. "I'm a big girl, Em. I can stay at the house by myself."

"Of course you can. But running a ranch takes a lot of work." Emery paused. "What about the horses?"

Ever since the accident, Gracie had developed a fear of horses. Especially her barrel-racing horse, Brandy. It was Brandy that had panicked when Cole's truck had almost hit them and thrown Gracie. Now Gracie couldn't be within ten feet of a horse without tremors racking her body. And if she couldn't be near a horse, she couldn't feed, water, and care for them.

"Maybe we could hire someone to do it," she said lamely, even though she knew that they didn't have the money for that.

"There's no need to hire someone." Carly pulled out her cellphone. "I'm sure Zane could send a ranch hand over to help with the horses."

Emery shook her head. "Cole wouldn't go for it. He hates asking people for help. And speaking of

Cole, we better get back to the ranch. I left him a text message about where we'd gone, but knowing his aversion to modern technology, he didn't think to look at his phone. I swear the man lives in the stone age."

"You do know my brother." Gracie laughed as she scooted to the end of the booth to grab her walker. "I need to go to the bathroom. I'll meet you out front." She hugged Carly goodbye before heading to the restrooms.

When she came out, Dirk was clearing the booth where they'd been sitting. She went to move past him, praying he was too busy to notice her, but he turned with the tub of dirty dishes at the last second and almost ran into her. He flashed his usual bright smile.

"Pardon me, Miss Gracie. I'm not as good at bussing as I am at flipping burgers."

She tried to act as nonchalant as possible, but it was hard when her cheeks burned with embarrassment. "Why are you bussing tables? I thought Jimmy did that."

"He called in sick this morning. No doubt due to the wedding punch I caught him and his buddies spiking." He glanced at the door. "Did Emery run off and leave you?"

"No, she's waiting outside." She didn't know what to say after that, and he didn't seem to know either. The kiss had obviously made them both uncomfortable, and she felt heartsick. She and Dirk had always been able to talk about anything, and she'd gone and ruined it.

After a few awkward seconds, Dirk ended her torture. "Well, I guess I'll catch you later." He stepped to the side to let her pass, and she suddenly noticed the Band-Aid on his neck. She couldn't help being concerned.

"What happened to your neck?"

His hand self-consciously covered the skin-colored bandage as his cheeks turned a bright red. She couldn't ever remember Dirk blushing. She did all the time, but never Dirk.

"Just a shaving nick." He backed away. "I better get back to cooking."

She watched him disappear into the kitchen and was confused. Not only because Dirk was acting so flustered, but also because the sexy scruff on his face didn't look like it had been shaved in a week.

"That boy sure has a way with the ladies."

Gracie turned to see Old Man Sims looking at the doorway to the kitchen. He grinned at her. "Reminds me of myself. I had all the girls in town baiting their hook to catch me." He paused. "Even Miss Lucy Arrington herself."

"You dated Lucy?"

He leaned closer and held a hand to his ear. "What's that?"

Gracie spoke louder. "Lucy? You dated Lucy Arrington?"

Mr. Sims nodded. "Yep. I sure did. She wasn't much of a talker, that one." He winked, his thick eyebrow moving up and down like a furry white caterpillar. "But there's no need to talk when there's better things to do."

Gracie couldn't hide her surprise. Not that Lucy had a lover. While the entire world thought her aunt had been a prudish old maid who spent her days writing, Gracie and Becky knew differently.

They'd found Lucy's diary and knew their aunt had a lover. They just never thought it was Old Man Sims. The man was ancient and had been married at least five times and had eleven kids and enough grandkids and great-grandkids to start his own town.

But now that she thought about it, it made sense. The man obviously had something that made all those women want to hop in bed with him and make babies. And if he had been that close to Lucy, maybe he would have some insight on where another chapter was hidden.

But before she could continue their conversation, a horn honked. She glanced out the large picture window to see Emery's car parked by the curb. "I need to go, Mr. Sims, but I'd love to hear more about how you and Lucy started dating."

Mr. Sims looked baffled. "What's that?"

She figured she could be here all day at this rate. She lifted a hand. "Talk with you soon." She reached the door just as a middle-aged cowboy was stepping in. When he saw her, he moved back outside and held the door for her.

Since she'd grown up in Bliss, she knew everyone in town. She even knew the truckers who only stopped for beer and wings at the Watering Hole on Twofer Tuesdays. But she didn't know this man. And yet, there was something familiar about his face when he doffed his hat and placed it over his heart.

"How do, pretty lady? It's certainly a gorgeous morning after all that rain, ain't it?"

"Yes, it is," she said as she moved out the door. "Are you new in town?"

He pulled his hat on and took a long drag of the cigarette wedged between his fingers. When he spoke, the smoke came out of his mouth like a puffing steam engine. "As new as a freshly minted penny." He flicked the cigarette to the ground and stomped it out with his boot heel before tipping his hat. "Have a good day, darlin'."

Gracie watched him disappear inside in a cloud of smoke and tried to figure out where she'd met him before.

*"Everyone assumed Johnny had come to town to choose a bride. But the entire time he smiled and gave directions to the boardinghouse, he kept his eye on the hired gunslinger Dax Davenport."*

# Chapter Four

❦

SOMETHING INSIDE OF DIRK TURNED feral when he noticed his daddy talking to Gracie. Before Holt's butt could hit the seat at the counter, Dirk was there to roughly grab his arm and guide him through the kitchen to the back door. Carly was too busy cooking to notice, but Ms. Marble stopped placing muffins on a plate as her gaze narrowed on Holt.

Dirk should've made the introductions. It wasn't like people wouldn't find out soon enough that Holt was his daddy. Especially when he had already told Mrs. Crawley so she'd let him into Dirk's room at the motor lodge. But if Dirk introduced him to Ms. Marble, she would have a lot of questions. And he didn't have time for that. He wanted his father gone. Now.

"I'm taking a break," he said as he guided his dad out the door. "I'll be back in five." Once in the alley, he released Holt and turned on him. "I thought you were leaving first thing this morning."

Holt flashed a smile. "Now is that any way to talk to your old man? Not that I'm that much older than you." He squinted his eyes. "What are you now? Twenty-seven? Twenty-eight?"

It wasn't surprising that he didn't know Dirk's age. Holt had never been concerned with his kids as much as he was concerned with himself. "Try twenty-four," Dirk said dryly.

He lifted both brows. "Really? I thought you was at least twenty-six. Or is that how old the triplets are now?"

"They're twenty-seven."

Holt shook his head. "Damn, it seems like only yesterday that I held those three little nuggets in my arms."

"And then promptly left my mama to take care of them."

"I came back, didn't I? I always come back."

"Only when you need money."

Holt pulled the pack of cigarettes from his front pocket and lipped one out. It bobbed as he talked. "You seem to have a selcctive memory, son." He pulled a lighter from his hip pocket and lit the cigarette, taking a deep drag before releasing the smoke at Dirk. "One time, I came back for my ornery son who was headed for the juvenile detention center until I volunteered to do my parental duty."

Dirk had been fifteen and wild as a March hare. His poor grandmother had done her best to raise him after the death of his mother. But the loss of his mom turned him into an angry, belligerent kid. And in high school he started releasing some of that anger by ditching school, smoking pot, and stealing cars and taking them for joyrides. One of those joyrides had landed him in the juvenile detention center. The judge thought he was giving Dirk a break by giving Holt custody. Instead, he had sentenced Dirk to hard time.

"I don't think parental duties include making your kid work to pay your gambling debts and drive you home after you'd been kicked out of bars," he said.

Holt shrugged. "I was merely teaching you how to be a responsible human being." He swept out a hand and smoke trailed behind it. "And just look at you now. Although I'm still trying to figure out why you're working at a greasy spoon diner when you own a company that makes—"

Dirk glanced over his shoulder at the door. "Would you keep it down?"

Holt smiled slyly. "And here I thought you hadn't learned anything from the time you spent with me. But it turns out you're a chip off the old block." He lowered his voice and leaned closer. "So what kind of scam are you running here, son? Are you going for the diner or much bigger fish?"

The last thing Dirk wanted was to be a chip off the old block. Unfortunately, he was running a scam and had been for the last six months. He just wasn't about to bring his father in on it.

"I gave you money," he said. "Now it's time for you to leave."

Holt studied him for a moment before he nodded. "I plan to, but you don't want your old dad hitting the road on an empty stomach, now do you?"

Holt had never worried about his son going hungry. Dirk had gone to bed hungry more times than he could count before he got his first job washing dishes. He started to point that out when the back door opened and Carly appeared. "Sorry to interrupt, Dirk, but I need you to bus tables. We're getting backed up."

"Sure. I'll be right there." He waited for the door to close before he turned to Holt. "Fine. I'll pay for your breakfast, but then I want you gone."

"Sure thing, son. I always hate to overstay my welcome."

It was a crock of crap. Holt always overstayed his welcome. Especially when he had a new audience to entertain. Dirk made sure to get his daddy's order up as quickly as possible, but Holt took his good sweet time eating the over-easy eggs and sausage as he regaled the people sitting at the counter with one story after another. Holt could sling bullshit better than most, which was exactly where Dirk had gotten it.

"Your dad is so funny, Dirk," Kelly the waitress said as she brought in a stack of dirty plates.

Carly stopped whisking eggs and turned to him. "That's your father? I thought he was just some guy you were doing odd jobs for. I didn't realize you were related."

"Then you didn't take a close enough look," Ms. Marble said as she wiped off the prep counter.

Dirk wasn't surprised that the older woman had figured things out. Ms. Marble was smart and observant. Of all the people in Bliss, he was closest to her. She was a retired teacher and an excellent baker who Carly had hired to bake for the diner.

But it wasn't her cookies that he loved so much as her kindness and generosity. She was the first person who had befriended him when he came to Bliss. And he felt guilty as hell for continuing to lie to her.

"So you think we look alike?" he asked.

"A little, but that wasn't what gave it away. Only spouses or relatives can bring out the kind of tension you've been displaying since your father arrived. I'm going to assume that you and he don't get along."

"That's an understatement."

She gave him a stern look. "That's still no excuse for bad manners. You should've introduced him to me and Carly." Ms. Marble was a stickler for proper etiquette.

"Yes, ma'am. I just thought that since he's leaving today, there would be no reason for introductions."

Carly set the whisk down and grabbed a dish-towel to wipe her hands. "Well, he's not leaving until I get a chance to meet him. While he's here, I intend to find out everything I can about the elusive Dirk Hadley." She hurried into the dining room.

*Great.* This was exactly why Dirk hadn't made introductions. He didn't want his cover blown. Fortunately, not even his father knew why he was really in Bliss.

"My mother was the one I didn't get along with," Ms. Marble said. "Probably because we were too much alike. We were both dreamers who thought love would conquer all. If I'd had more of my daddy's logical way of thinking, my life might've turned out less painful. Although I guess we learn from hard times much more than we learn from good."

If that were the case, then Dirk had done his share of learning.

By the time Carly got back to the kitchen, he'd filled six orders and Ms. Marble had left to water her tomato plants.

"Your daddy is a charmer with the women just like you are," Carly said. "He asked me to marry him two seconds after meeting me—of course, Kelly said he'd already proposed to her."

That was his daddy. A real ladies' man.

Dirk stacked granola pancakes on a plate. "So what interesting facts did you learn about me?"

Carly washed her hands and dried them. "Not a one. Every time I asked him a question about you, he'd go off on some other story." She picked up the plate of pancakes and carried it to the prep counter where she added a scoop of cinnamon butter and a small carafe of maple syrup. "It sounds like he's had as many jobs as you've had."

Holt had. But unlike Dirk, he'd been fired from every single one. "Yes, he's a jack of all trades, my daddy." He scooped some scrambled eggs onto a flour tortilla on a plate and added fried potatoes before handing it to her.

She took the breakfast burrito and added grated cheese and her homemade salsa. "That's good to hear because I hired him to help you out here in the diner while I'm in Atlanta."

Dirk set down his spatula and turned to her. "What?"

She placed the order on the pass-through and rang the bell. "I feel bad leaving you here to manage the diner after you just finished managing it while Zane and I went on our honeymoon. Your father can help cook, wash dishes, and bus tables."

Dirk shook his head. "Believe me, Carly. You do not want to hire my dad."

"Why not? He told me he taught you everything you know."

That was true. He had taught Dirk everything he knew, including how to lie and scam people.

"It's just not a good idea," he said.

She studied him for only a second, before she nodded. "Okay, I get it. You don't want to work with your dad. I wouldn't want to work with mine either. I'll see if the Sanders sisters can help you out while I'm gone. But I hate telling your father that I can't hire him. He looked so happy when I asked."

"I'll take care of it." Dirk headed into the diner.

Holt was still holding court. People had gathered around his barstool as he told a story about a long-shot horse that had won him thousands. If it was true, he'd spent the money as soon as he got it.

When he saw Dirk, he stopped talking and smiled. "There's my boy."

Dirk nodded at the door. "I need to talk to you."

"Of course." Holt finished off his coffee before he got to his feet and grabbed his cowboy hat. "If y'all will excuse me, it looks like I need to have a father-son talk." He followed Dirk out of the diner. As soon as they were outside, he took out his pack of cigarettes. "I'm glad you got me out of there. I needed a smoke in a bad way."

"I didn't get you out here for a smoke." Dirk headed to the curb where Holt's beat-up pickup truck was parked next to the handicapped parking sign. He walked around the front and pulled open the driver's side door. "Time to leave, Daddy."

Holt took his time lighting a cigarette before he strolled over to where Dirk stood. "I'm sorry, son, but I can't leave now. I just got myself a job."

"Not anymore. You won't be working at the diner."

Holt only shrugged before he leaned against his truck. "I'm not much help in the kitchen anyway." He took another puff and glanced around. "When I first drove into this town, I thought Spring had given me the wrong information, because who in their right mind would want to live in this shithole?"

Dirk had wondered how his daddy had found him. He should've known it was his sister Spring who had told him. She had always talked too fast and too much. "You shouldn't be bugging my sisters."

"I wouldn't have had to if that old bat you have for a grandmother had told me where you were. Instead, when I called, she gave me an hour lecture on being a good role model." He took a deep drag of his cigarette. "Dads aren't supposed to be role models. That's what pro athletes are for. Of course, you never were any good at sports." He glanced over and grinned. "But you always were good at sniffing out ways to make money."

"There's no money to be made in this town, Holt."

Holt's eyebrows lifted beneath the brim of his hat. "Now that's not what I just heard from the townsfolk. They seem to think that there's a treasure hidden in Bliss."

Dirk felt his neck muscles tense, but he kept his voice steady. "Not a treasure. Just an old book."

Holt tipped his head back and blew perfect smoke rings up into the clear blue sky. "Would the chapters in your motel room safe be from that same old book?"

Dirk clenched his fists to keep from grabbing Holt by the shirt and shaking him. "You broke into my safe?"

"Not broke. Just kept trying family birth dates until I stumbled upon the right one. I should've known it would be your mama's. You were always a mama's boy."

It was hard for Dirk to keep his voice steady. "Those chapters aren't mine. They belong to the Arringtons. So there's no money to be made there."

Holt studied him for a long moment, and Dirk knew his mind was feverishly working to find an angle. It didn't take long for a smile to curve his lips.

"No, but I bet one of them online news folks would pay me a pretty penny to find out about those chapters."

*"Daisy had everything worked out. The supplies and horse she'd bought were waiting for her at the stables. Now all she needed to do was sneak out of town without being caught."*

# CHAPTER FIVE

❧

"STOP BEING RIDICULOUS, COLE," GRACIE said as she slowly made her way to the chicken coop. "I'll be fine staying here by myself for a week while you go to Atlanta."

"You just left the rehab center." Cole followed her like a mother hen. "What if you have a relapse?"

She repeated what her doctors and therapists had told her—even though she didn't completely believe it herself. "I don't have a disease, Cole. I ruptured a disk and bruised my spine and my body is recovering from that injury. There's no way I'm going to have a relapse if I keep doing my therapy." When she reached the coop, Delilah and Debbie flew down from their roosts to greet her. "Good morning, ladies," she said as she reached for the coop door. Cole beat her to it and held it while she maneuvered her walker inside.

"Just another reason I shouldn't leave. You

thought of any excuse to skip your therapy right after the accident, which is exactly why you didn't start to heal sooner. And I'm not going to let that happen again."

After the accident, Gracie hadn't wanted to do her therapy. She hadn't wanted to do anything. Not only had she been grieving for Hef and losing the use of her legs, but she'd also been grieving for her mother.

A couple weeks before the accident, her mom had shown up at the ranch. Ava had needed money, and she knew she could get it from Hef. That was the reason Cole had been driving so fast and almost hit Gracie and Brandy. He'd just found out that Hef had given Ava all the money they'd been saving for the horse ranch.

Gracie had been upset about the money too, but she was more upset about her mother being in town and never once asking to see her. Gracie had been at college, but Austin was only an hour away from Bliss. One measly hour, and her mother couldn't even make the effort to see her only daughter.

Her mother's lack of interest on top of the accident and losing her stepfather had sent her into a deep depression. She'd tried to put on a brave front for Cole, but inside, she'd felt dead and hopeless . . . until Dirk had shown up.

He'd arrived at the ranch like a ray of sunshine on a frigid day, his bright smile cracking open the hard shell of her despair. When he offered to do odd jobs around the ranch in exchange for her old Chevy Malibu, she'd latched onto him like a lifeline. He brought her chickens, told her funny stories about all the jobs he'd had over the years, and treated her like a normal person instead of an invalid. And in return, she'd told him the story of her life.

She told him about her mama bringing her to the ranch when she was just a baby. About Cole's daddy adopting her after her mama ran off, even though she wasn't his flesh and blood. She told him about how Cole had taken her under his wing and taught her how to fish and skip rocks and ride a horse. She told him about reading the first Tender Heart book and how Lucy's words had made her feel so proud to be part of the Arrington family. She confided almost everything to Dirk, except her love. Now she'd even confided that.

"I'm not going to stop doing therapy." She pulled dried corn from the plastic grocery bag she'd hooked to her walker and sprinkled it to the chickens. "In fact, I just got off the phone with my new physical therapist. He'll be here Thursday morning." She glanced over in time to see Cole's brow knit with concern.

She knew why. With therapy came more bills, and he was already struggling to pay the hospital and rehabilitation bills she'd incurred. If not for her, Cole would have his horse ranch up and running by now.

"But that still leaves the horses to take care of," Cole said. "And I refuse to have Zane send over someone from his ranch. You know how I feel about charity."

Gracie wanted to offer to take care of the horses, but knew she couldn't. Just the thought of being close to a horse made her break out in a cold sweat.

Which was a ridiculous reaction to have when you lived on a ranch.

She finished feeding the chickens and maneuvered out of the coop. "Please let Zane send someone over to help, Cole," she pleaded. "If not for yourself, then for Emery. She deserves to have a honeymoon."

Cole glanced back at the porch where Emery was sitting in a rocker doing some edits on the non-fiction mail-order bride book she was getting ready for publication. She glanced up and smiled, and that was all it took for Cole to concede. "Fine. I'll go. But I'm not taking help from Zane for free. I'll pay one of his ranch hands extra to come by and take care of the horses."

"Yay!" She leaned over her walker and hugged him. "Now go tell your wife the good news."

Gracie collected the eggs from her chickens while Cole talked with Emery. Her squeal of delight said it all. Once Cole had left for Emmett's gas station, Gracie made her way to the porch.

"So what did you say to change his mind?" Emery asked.

Gracie moved up the ramp Cole had built for her when she was in the wheelchair. "All I did was mention how much you wanted a honeymoon. It was his love for you that clinched the deal." She sat down in the rocker next to Emery's. "So how is the editing going?"

"Slowly. While you were gone, I put an ad in the local paper for mail-order bride diaries. I thought I'd get just a few, but I ended up getting close to twenty. And with the ones I already have, there's way too many entries to use in one book. So I'm

having to sort through them, choose the ones I
like, and then place them into a cohesive story that
depicts the life of a mail-order bride."

"That sounds like a lot of work."

"A lot of work for little money," Emery stared at
the screen of her laptop and frowned. "I'm starting
to think I should put the book on hold and start
taking more editing jobs to help pay the bills."

"Didn't you get an advance for the book?"

"Yes, but Cole and I agreed that the money
should go to the families of the brides who kept
diaries. I'm only taking a percentage of the royalties for editing."

Gracie understood why Cole felt that way. He
was still mad that Lucy had left all her royalties to
the Texas library system instead of her family. The
only book she hadn't mentioned in her will was the
last Tender Heart book. Gracie knew in her heart
that Lucy wanted that book to go to her family.
Cole's portion of the royalties would be more than
enough to pay her medical bills and help build his
stables. Now all they needed to do was find it.

"Have you thought of any more places to look
for chapters?" she asked.

A sparkle entered Emery's eyes. "I think we have
a lot more places to look." She set her laptop down
on the table and leaned closer. "I got the results
back from my friend. Like we thought, the envelopes are no more than five years old."

Gracie's heart thumped with excitement, but she
was also confused. "So someone found the book
after Lucy died, then decided to hide each chapter
separately decades later? But why? Why wouldn't
they just sell the book when they found it and

make a fortune?"

"I don't know, but if that's what happened, then it's likely that chapters could be somewhere that's already been searched." She picked up the notepad and red pencil sitting on the table and started writing. "We've found a chapter in the chapel where Lucy first got inspiration for the Tender Heart series." She moved to the next line. "One in the diner where she wrote all of her book outlines. One in the cemetery where she got inspiration for her characters. And one in Zane and Becky's bunkhouse."

"The bunkhouse? Why there?"

"Carly and I discovered a picture of Lucy in the bunkhouse in a box of photos Ms. Marble loaned Carly for the diner. We think Lucy might've been in love with one of the cowboys who worked for the Arringtons and gone there to meet him."

The name popped out of Gracie's mouth before she could stop it. "Honey Bee."

Emery glanced up from the notepad. "Excuse me?"

Gracie had promised Becky that she wouldn't tell anyone about Lucy's diary, but Emery wasn't just anyone. She was her sister-in-law, and she knew how to keep a secret. She'd proven that by not telling anyone about Gracie trying to pass off her own writing as Lucy's. And if the diary would help find the other chapters, Emery should know about it.

"Honey Bee was the name Lucy gave her lover when she wrote about him in her diary."

Emery stood up so fast that she sent the rocker slamming back into the porch wall. "Lucy had a diary? Where is it? Can I read it?"

"I can't show it to you without Becky's permission. We found it when we were teenagers and made a pact to keep it a secret. But I'm sure Becky will let you read it . . . as long as you promise not to tell anyone. If the press got their hands on it, they'd no doubt exploit it."

Emery sat down on the edge of her chair. "But you can't mean to keep Lucy's diary a secret forever. It's a special piece of history that needs to be shared with her readers so they can get a glimpse of the amazing mind that created Tender Heart."

"Umm . . . well, it's not about her everyday thoughts." Gracie felt her face heat. "It's more about the sex she had with Honey Bee."

Emery's eyebrows lifted. "You mean in detail." When Gracie nodded, she sat back in the chair and stared out at the ranch. "Then I can understand why you want to keep it a secret. That's a little more personal than the mail order brides talking about how they churned butter." She glanced at Gracie. "Did she say who Honey Bee was?"

"No, but we found the diary in the old Reed house. So we think whoever it was lived there at one time. Has Mr. Sims ever mentioned living there?"

"Old Man Sims? You think he was Lucy's Honey Bee?"

"He mentioned dating her when we were in the diner the other day. And he did seem to have a way with the ladies when he was younger." She paused as a thought struck her. "Do you think he's the one hiding the chapters?"

"It's possible. We need to find out if he ever worked for the Earhart Ranch and lived in the bunkhouse. And if he ever rented the Reed place. In the meantime, we need to look at the Reed place for another chapter. Do you think Becky would give us permission to look when I get back from Atlanta?"

"I know she would, but why do we need to wait until you get back? I could go over and look while you're gone. And I could look other places too. The faster we find the book, the faster Cole can get his horse ranch."

Emery's expression was skeptical, but she nodded. "Okay, but don't mention it to Cole. He wouldn't be happy if he knew you were running around the countryside looking for the rest of the chapters while we're gone. Not only does he worry about you, but he thinks searching for the book is a waste of time. Which is why I've decided not to tell him anything until we've found the entire book."

It was doubtful that Cole's skepticism was the real reason Emery wanted to wait. It was more likely that she didn't want him to be disappointed like he'd been when he found out Gracie had forged the first version of the lost manuscript. But Cole wouldn't be disappointed this time. Gracie was going to make sure of it.

"We'll find them, Em," she vowed.

They continued to brainstorm about possible places to look for the chapters, and Emery wrote all their ideas down on the notepad, including the three ranches owned by the Arrington cousins.

The Arrington Ranch had once been one huge ranch that included thousands of acres of land and head of cattle. But when Zane, Raff, and Cole's fathers disagreed on how to run the ranch, they ended up splitting it into three separate ranches. The Tender Heart Ranch which was now owned by Raff, the Earhart Ranch which was owned by Zane, and the Arrington Ranch which was owned by Cole.

Since Cole and Gracie lived in the same house that Lucy Arrington had lived and written her novels in, it made sense that a chapter would be there. But Gracie had thoroughly searched the Arrington Ranch after she'd found the first chapter and had come up empty handed. So Emery crossed their ranch off the list.

That left Zane's and Raff's ranches.

"We already found a chapter in Zane's bunkhouse," Emery said. "But I think we need to thoroughly search the Earhart ranch house since that was where Lucy was born and the house is the template for the ranch house in her Tender Heart series. Since Carly lives there, she can search it." She glanced at the list. "What about Raff's ranch?"

Gracie shook her head. "I don't think anything there has a connection to Lucy. The house and barn were built after Lucy died, right after the Arrington Ranch was divided between her nephews. And a couple years ago, that house was destroyed in a fire. That's why Raff lives in the old cabin when he's in town."

"Raff certainly travels a lot. I've never even met him."

Gracie smiled at the thought of her wandering cousin. "He'll be back. He always comes back."

Emery tore off the page from the notebook and handed it to her. "Promise you'll only search the places you feel comfortable with. When we get back, Carly and I can help with the others."

She folded the paper in half. "I promise. Can I use your car while you're gone?"

"Of course, you can use my car, but it's a stick. It might be easier to drive yours since it's an automatic."

Gracie stared at her in surprise. "Mine? I don't have my car anymore. I gave it to Dirk for all the work he did here on the ranch."

"Well, he refused to take it. He said he wanted to leave it here for you so you'd have something to drive when you got back." Emery reached out and squeezed Gracie's hand. "He's a good friend who never doubted that you'd walk again."

Dirk had been a good friend . . . until Gracie had ruined it with one kiss. Now she had to figure out how to fix her mistake.

She reached for her walker. "Where did Cole put my car keys? I need to make a trip into town."

*"Johnny was standing in the side alley by the boardinghouse waiting for Dax to come out of the saloon when he heard a mumbled curse. He glanced up in time to see a pile of petticoats sailing toward him."*

# Chapter Six

❦

THE KNOCK ON THE DOOR woke Dirk from a sound sleep. He blinked awake. Sunlight poured in through the open cowboy-print curtains of his room at the motor lodge. He sat up and looked at the analog clock on the nightstand. The face had a picture of a cowboy on it, the hands the cowboy's legs. At the moment, those spotted cowhide chaps were doing the splits. 3:15. He'd napped for over an hour. Having to get up at four in the morning to answer emails before he headed to the diner screwed up a good night's sleep.

He closed the laptop he'd been working on before he'd fallen asleep and slid it in the nightstand drawer. It had a passcode so he wasn't worried about Winnie being able to get into his business emails and documents when she cleaned his room. Of course, he'd thought that he had a good passcode for the room safe too, and his father had cracked that.

Just the thought of Holt made Dirk angry. It had taken a couple thousand dollars to get his father to promise to keep his mouth shut. Not that a promise from Holt was worth a penny.

He took his time pulling on his jeans before he walked to the door. It was probably Winnie. Since he drove her home from Becky's wedding, she had been convinced that he had a thing for her. She now stopped by the diner and bugged him on a daily basis and had recently started leaving sexual notes on his pillow after she cleaned his room. He hated hurting a woman's feelings, but it looked like he didn't have much choice.

He pulled the door open. "Look, Winnie—" He cut off when he saw Gracie. She was dressed in boots, jeans, and a tank top with a scooped neck just low enough to show off a hint of soft cleavage. Her light blond hair hung around her shoulders in thick waves of lemony sunshine and her cheeks were flushed a pretty pink.

"I'm sorry," she said. "I didn't mean to wake you."

Up until now, he'd kept his word to Cole and avoided Gracie whenever she came into town. But there was no way to avoid her when she was standing at his door.

He ran a hand through his mussed hair. "It's no big deal. I was just resting up before I have to go back to the diner."

"I guess you're extra busy now that Carly is gone. That must be . . ." Her gaze lowered to his bare chest. "Hard."

He thought about grabbing a shirt. Her eyes

had always felt like turquoise lasers that could cut straight through to his soul. He crossed his arms over his chest and cleared his throat. "I don't mind the extra work. It keeps me busy. Speaking of the diner, I better get back over there and get ready for the dinner rush." He paused. "Did you need something?"

She reached into the side pocket of the purse that was hooked over one handle of her walker and pulled out a set of keys. "I brought your car."

Dirk glanced over her shoulder and saw the old Chevy Malibu parked in the parking lot. "I don't want your car, Miss Gracie."

She held out the keys. "We had a deal. And you certainly held up your end of the bargain with all the work you did on the ranch."

"I didn't do that much. I built a little ol' chicken coop and cut down some weeds. I'd do that for any friend."

She lowered the keys, and her big eyes shimmered with something that scared Dirk shitless. "Are we friends?"

If it hadn't been for that gut-wrenching shimmer, he could've continued to keep his distance. But women's tears were Dirk's kryptonite. He caved like a hornet's nest beneath a boot heel.

"Of course we're friends. Why would you think otherwise?"

She blinked, and if one tear fell, he knew he was toast and would have no choice but to pull her into his arms and comfort her. Luckily, she held those tears in. Which, for some reason, made him feel even more gutted. "Because of the kiss."

He didn't want to talk about the kiss. He'd spent

way too much time thinking about it. Even now, he had a hard time keeping his gaze from her sweet, full lips that had tasted like autumn peaches and . . . innocence. It was that innocence he was trying to protect. That innocence that kept him from telling the truth about their kiss.

"Oh, that little kiss?" he said in his best good ol' boy voice. "Why that was no big deal. And it certainly wasn't something that could end a friendship. Things happen at weddings. People get a little juiced and do stupid things."

*Stupid?* Shit, he was really screwing this up. "Not that the kiss was stupid. Like I said at the time, it was real nice." She visibly cringed, and he tried to search for a better word. "Real nice and . . . sweet." It had been sweet. And Dirk had always had a sweet tooth. But, in this instance, he couldn't indulge his craving.

He held out a hand. "Friends?"

She hesitated for only a second before she let go of the walker and took his hand. "Friends." She held up the keys in her other hand. "But only if you take your car."

"No can do, Miss Gracie. You'll need that car while Emery and Cole are gone." He nodded at the Subaru parked right out front. "Besides, Carly left me her car."

She released an annoyed huff. "You are the most stubborn man I know, Dirk Hadley." She shoved the keys in her purse so hard that it tipped the walker.

Dirk caught the walker before it could knock into Gracie, but not before her purse slipped off the handle. It hit the cement and all the paraphernalia women carry in their purses spilled out across the walkway.

"Shit!" Gracie said.

Dirk had never heard Gracie cuss before. He sent her a startled look before he broke out in laughter. "You do seem to carry around a lot of that in your purse." He couched down and started picking things up.

Gracie joined him. She sat rather than crouched, but being able to lower to the ground showed how strong her legs had become. He understood her motivation for wanting to help when she quickly grabbed the scattered tampons. Once they were safely in her purse, she reached for the journal he held.

"Secret diary?" he asked as he handed it to her.

Her cheeks brightened. "No, just a silly story I started when I was at the rehabilitation center."

"I didn't know you liked to write. Are you going to be the next Lucy in the Arrington family?"

Her blush grew deeper. "I could never be that good."

It bothered him that Gracie thought so little of her abilities. He wondered if it was the accident or if she'd always been so unsure of herself. "I think you could do anything you set your mind to." He handed her a couple of pens. "So what's this story about?"

"Just a young woman."

"What does this woman do? Does she run away from home and join the circus? Travel to another planet and become their goddess? Kiss a frog and turn him into a prince?" He didn't know why he threw in the last part.

She reached for her wallet. "She goes on a quest to find her mom."

The premise hit way too close to home. He glanced at her, but she wasn't looking at him with a calculated look, and he realized his mistake. She wasn't talking about him. She was talking about herself. Gracie had told him about her mother deserting her as a baby. She was writing a story about her life. And more importantly, her desire to have a mom. He understood. He understood completely.

"And does she find her?" he asked.

"Of course," she said softly. "I love happy endings."

If anyone got a happy ending, he hoped it was Gracie. He handed over her sunglasses. "Well, when you have it finished, I'd like to read it. Quests have always hooked me."

"I doubt I'll ever finish it." She studied him. "And even if I do, you'll be long gone by then."

He allowed himself to get lost in her Caribbean-blue eyes for only a moment before he went back to collecting her things. Once her purse was filled to the brim, he took it from her and helped her up.

"You want me to drive you home?" he asked. "I can hitch back."

"No, thank you. You need to get to the diner, remember?" She took her purse and hooked the strap over the handle. "And I'll expect you to come get the car after Carly returns from Atlanta." She turned the walker and headed to her car. He should've let her go. But letting Gracie go was proving much more difficult than he had expected.

He followed her and opened the driver's door.

"I enjoy hitching rides. I meet a lot of nice folks that way." He waited for her to climb in before he took the walker and folded it. "You want this in the trunk?"

"The backseat is fine."

He placed it in the backseat, then slammed the door and waited as she started the car and rolled down the window. "I'll see you around, Miss Gracie."

She looked up at him, and it was like they were back at the Arrington Ranch and she was sitting in her wheelchair watching him as he went about his work. Every time he'd glanced over, she'd had the same look of adoration he saw on her face now. It made him feel ten feet tall. It also made him feel like the lowest form of slime on earth. It was almost a relief when Winnie came hurrying down the walkway pushing her cleaning cart at a break-neck pace.

"Dirk!" The cart hit a crack in the cement and all the cleaning supplies jostled before she pulled to a stop right in front of Gracie's car. She sashayed straight over to Dirk. Her jeans were so tight they looked painted on, and her t-shirt was two sizes too small. The words *Bliss Motor Lodge* were distorted and stretched out over her big breasts. She pressed those breasts against him as she looped her arms around his neck.

"I was hopin' to catch you nappin' so we could have some snuggle time before you had to go back to work." She shot Gracie a sly glance through her heavily mascaraed lashes. "Sorta like we did on Saturday night." She brushed a long-nail over the spot where she'd given him a hickey. "Oh, no." She stuck out her bottom lip in a pout. "Your Winnie mark is all gone. I guess I'll just have to give you another."

He had never gotten mean with a woman in his life, but Winnie certainly deserved a setting down for her aggressive and inappropriate behavior. He could tell by Gracie's widened eyes that she believed every word.

He started to unhook Winnie's claws from around his neck and explain things to Gracie when a thought struck him. What was he doing? If Gracie thought that he and Winnie had something going on, maybe she'd stop looking at him like he was someone special. Maybe she'd realize that he didn't deserve her.

He wrapped his arm around Winnie's generous waist and pulled her closer. "You can mark me all you want, darlin', as long as I get to do the same. And as for snugglin', I've got a little time before I have to be at the diner." He nodded at Gracie. "See you later, Miss Gracie."

Her eyes held such gut-wrenching heartbreak that he almost released Winnie and confessed all his sins. Every last one of them. But that would cause Gracie even more pain, so instead, he headed back to his room with Winnie in tow. The door had barely closed shut behind them when he heard the squeal of tires as Gracie peeled out of the parking lot.

He released Winnie and opened the door. "Time for you to go."

Her fingernails trailed down his chest. "What do you mean it's time for me to go? I thought we were going to have some fun."

He removed her hands. "Now you know I can't have any fun with you, Winnie. Not if I want to keep my place of residence." He maneuvered her out the door. "And don't worry about cleaning my room today. I can make my own bed."

Her eyes narrowed. "Why you good-for-nothing, lousy jerk!" she yelled. "You only used me to make Gracie Arrington jealous. Fuck you, Dirk Hadley, and the little horse you rode in on." She whirled and pushed her cart hell-bent-for-leather down the walkway. When she was gone, he heaved a sigh of relief. It only lasted a second. As soon as an image of Gracie's face flashed in his mind, he didn't feel relieved. He felt like an asshole.

Of course, it was better to hurt her now than later.

He turned to go back to his room when he noticed a folded piece of paper lying on the cement. It had probably fallen off of Winnie's cart and was another X-rated note she planned to leave on his pillow. He picked it up and turned back to his room, intending to toss it in the trash like he'd tossed the other ones. But before he did, he unfolded it to make sure.

He didn't find a list of the sexual things Winnie wanted to do to him. He found a list of locations. And at the top of the list were words that made the list even more intriguing.

*Places Tender Heart Chapters Might Be Hidden.*

*"Falling into a cowboy's arms was not on Daisy's list of adventures she wanted to have . . . even if the cowboy had the prettiest blue eyes she'd ever seen. She sent him an innocent look. 'Oh goodness. I guess I leaned a little too far out the window.'"*

# CHAPTER SEVEN

WINNIE!

Gracie's hands tightened on the steering wheel as she drove back to the ranch. How could Dirk be interested in Winnie Crawley? The woman was the most mean-spirited person in Bliss. She had no manners, no morals, and no love for anyone but herself. And if Dirk couldn't see that, then he wasn't the man she thought he was. While the rest of the town had always viewed Dirk as a carefree drifter who wanted no responsibilities or ties, Gracie had looked beneath the easygoing smile and thought she'd seen a man who took life much more seriously than he was letting on. Obviously, she'd been wrong. If he took life seriously, he wouldn't be swapping hickeys with Winnie.

She cringed. To think she'd believed him when he'd said he'd nicked himself shaving. He'd probably laughed his butt off about fooling naïve Miss Gracie. Well, she might be naïve, but she was also the type of person who learned from her mistakes, and wasting her time dreaming about Dirk Hadley had been a huge mistake. One she didn't intend to make again.

She had much better things to do with her time. Like concentrating on finding the other Tender Heart chapters. She waited until she was off the highway and on the dirt road that led to the ranch before she pulled her cellphone out of her purse and called Becky.

Becky answered after the first ring. "Thank God you called! I'm trying to surprise Mason by cooking dinner tonight and my potatoes just exploded in the microwave."

Gracie was surprised. Not over the exploding potatoes, but over the fact that her friend was even attempting to cook. Becky hated cooking. Which proved how much she loved Mason.

"Did you prick holes in them with a fork first?" she asked.

"Shoot! I forgot about the fork pricking. I knew I should've taken notes when Carly gave me her recipe for twice-baked potatoes. It looks like we're going to have mashed potatoes tonight."

Gracie knew Becky well enough to know that she wasn't kidding. "Don't you dare serve Mason potatoes you scraped out of the microwave. Try again, and this time, poke the potatoes first."

"Fine. But if this fails, I'm ordering Italian. That's the one perk of big city life. Takeout."

Gracie laughed. "Well, don't get too attached to Austin. I don't want you liking it so much that you decide to live there permanently."

"Not a chance. We're only staying long enough for Mason to close down his law practice and then we'll be home. I can't wait to start buying cattle for our ranch and to fix up the old Reed house."

The mention of Becky's new house brought Gracie to the purpose of the phone call. "Speaking of the old Reed house, would you mind if I went over there and looked at the diary?"

"Of course not. The diary is as much yours as it is mine. But why? You've read that diary so many times, you should know it by heart."

"Actually, it's not the diary I want to look at as much as the hiding place in the floor." She paused for dramatic effect. "More chapters have been found of the last book."

Becky reacted like she thought she would. "Holy crap! How many? Who found them? And where?"

Gracie told her everything she'd learned from Emery, including how the envelopes had been tested and Emery's belief that the chapters had been hidden long after Lucy's death.

"So she thinks that someone is going around hiding them in places that Lucy frequented?" Becky asked.

"Or places that influenced her writing." She paused. "Or her life."

"Honey Bee," Becky said.

"That's exactly what I'm thinking. After you told me about the diary being taken out of the house when Mason was living there and then returned, I got to thinking. What if the person who took it is the same person who is hiding the chapters?"

"You're thinking they hid a chapter when they

returned the diary?"

"It's possible. When you checked beneath the floorboards for the diary, did you see anything?"

"No, but then I didn't look. I was only interested in the diary." Becky's voice grew excited. "Wouldn't it be so cool if a chapter was hidden in the floor with the diary?" She paused. "Maybe I should come back to Bliss and help you look. Austin is only an hour away."

Gracie didn't know why she wasn't more excited about the prospect of Becky's help. Maybe because finding another chapter would relieve some of her guilt about forging Lucy's book.

"Absolutely not," she said. "Technically, you and Mason are on your honeymoon. I won't have you leaving him to come help me look for a silly book."

The "silly book" made Becky read right through her ploy. She laughed. "Okay, I get it. You want to go on this treasure hunt by yourself. But you better save some chapters for me to find with you. You're not the only Tender Heart geek in the family. I'll call Zane and tell him you're coming by for the key. And I'll text you the security code. After the diary went missing, Mason installed an alarm."

"Thanks, Beck."

"No problem, but you better call me if you find something. Right now I need to explode some more potatoes."

After Becky hung up, Gracie thought about heading straight over to Zane's for the key to the house. But her new therapist was stopping by for her first physical therapy session.

Calvin had been recommended by one of her doctors at the rehabilitation center. He lived just south of Austin and was willing to come out to the ranch for their sessions. On the phone, he seemed nice but no nonsense. He'd asked her multiple questions about her injury, the therapy she'd done at the rehab center, and what exercises she was doing now. She had fudged a little on the latter. Since coming home, she hadn't worked as hard as she should've and was nervous about Calvin's first evaluation.

When Gracie pulled up the drive, she thought Calvin had beat her to the ranch. A beat-up old truck was parked in front. But she realized her mistake when a man came out of the barn. Surprisingly, it was the same man she'd met in front of the diner.

Cole had said that Zane was going to send over a ranch hand, but she'd thought it would be one of the ranch hands she knew. Certainly not a complete stranger. She thought about calling Zane and asking him to send someone she was more comfortable with, but then decided she was being silly. Especially when the man seemed so nice. As soon as she got out of the car, he smiled brightly and walked over to greet her.

"Howdy again. I didn't realize that you were the pretty miss I'd be helping out."

Gracie opened the back door to get her walker. "So you got a job working for Zane?"

"Hired on just yesterday. I guess with his sister married off, he needed an extra hand. Let me help you with that." He took the walker from her. "You must be Gracie. My mama's middle name was Grace and my daddy always called her Delia Gracie when he was happy. Of course, I can't repeat what he called her when he wasn't." He placed the cigarette he held in his hand between his teeth and snapped open the walker. "There you go, little lady." The lit cigarette bobbing in his mouth caught her attention.

"You weren't smoking in the barn, were you?" Barns burned down all the time by someone smoking too close to dry hay.

The smile slipped for a second as he pulled the cigarette from his mouth. "No, ma'am. I just lit one on the way out." The cigarette seemed too short to be just lit. But she couldn't very well accuse him of lying. She was relieved when he dropped the cigarette and ground it out with his heel. "But if you have a problem with smoking, I certainly wouldn't want to offend."

"Thank you." She paused. "And your name is?"

"Holt. Holt Hadley."

Gracie froze. She didn't have to ask if he was related to Dirk. She knew he was. That's why he'd seemed so familiar. It wasn't his features. He didn't have pretty gray eyes or a perfect nose or kissable lips. Or even a sexy smile. It was more the way he carried himself with a confidence that bordered on cockiness. Except on Holt, it seemed more forced and less genuine.

"By that shocked look, I'd say you're acquainted with my son Dirk." He winked. "He's always had a way with the pretty ladies."

After what had just happened with Winnie, she was more than a little annoyed by the comment. "Yes, he does seem to like the ladies."

Holt laughed. "Stung ya, did he?" He leaned a little closer. Too close. "You don't have to worry about that with me. I'm a one-woman man." Before she could deal with Dirk's dad making a pass at her, he changed the subject. "So this was where that Lucy Arrington lived and wrote all them novels?" He glanced around. "I gotta tell you this place don't look like it belonged to a rich author."

Gracie bristled. "Working ranches aren't usually glamorous, Mr. Hadley."

He looked back at her and grinned. "It's just Holt. You're a feisty little thing, ain't ya? I bet you'd be a real hellcat in the bedroom." He glanced down. "Or is that broke too?"

Gracie was struck speechless. Before she could think of a reply, a blue Chevy Equinox came up the drive and parked next to her car. The man who got out was dressed in jeans and a navy polo with *Lone Star Health* stitched over the pocket.

"Well, it looks like you've got company. I better get back to the Earhart Ranch." Holt tipped his cowboy hat. "But if you need anything . . . I mean anything at all, you let ol' Holt know. I'll be here every morning and every night."

Gracie should say something. She should call him out on his insult. Or fire him. But the fact that he was Dirk's father kept her from doing either. She watched him walk to his truck and wondered how he could be related to Dirk. Then she thought of Winnie's hickey and realized that maybe he and Dirk weren't that different. Maybe her love for Dirk had blinded her to his faults.

"Hello." The man in the navy polo walked over. He was younger than she expected and . . . cuter. He had deep brown eyes and a genuine smile. "You must be Gracie." He shifted the duffel bag he carried and held out a hand.

She took it. "And you must be Calvin."

"Yes, ma'am." He glanced briefly at the walker. "Where shall we get to work?"

Calvin wasn't kidding when he said they were going to get to work. Once she changed into her workout clothes, he put her through a vigorous routine of stretches and muscle-strengthening exercises. After she was sweating and exhausted, she fell back on the yoga mat he'd spread out on the living room floor.

"No more."

He scribbled something down on the clipboard. "Good job. Your muscles are much stronger than I expected. And I must admit that I'm curious as to why you still use a walker."

It was obvious he'd talked with some of her therapists at the rehabilitation center. She sat up and answered a little belligerently. "So I won't fall."

"But falling is part of learning to walk." His eyebrows lifted. "Ask any one-year-old."

Her face heated with anger more than embarrassment. "One-year-olds are expected to fall. Twenty-two-years olds aren't."

"They are if their body has suffered a trauma like yours has." He set down his clipboard and studied her with his somber brown eyes. "But I don't think you're afraid of falling, Gracie. I think you're more afraid of standing."

"Excuse me?"

He rested his arms on his bent knees. "I see it all the time in my line of work. People who suffer serious injuries lose months of their lives to surgeries and recovery. When they finally get back to their lives, they feel uncomfortable and unsure of who they are and how they fit into the world. So they cling to the crutches they were given during their recovery—wheelchairs, walkers—even when they don't need them anymore. They fear that their accident has changed them forever and they won't be able to go back to their old lives. If they're still in recovery, they won't have to."

She stared at him, too stunned to say a word.

Calvin picked up his clipboard and got to his feet. "I think we've had enough for today. Keep up your exercise and I'll see you in a couple days." He grabbed his duffel bag and headed for the door, but he stopped before he got there and turned to her. "Trust yourself, Gracie. You're stronger than you think."

*"Daisy McNeil was as innocent looking as a school girl with her big ol' brown eyes and pouting lips, but Johnny knew a con artist when he saw one. Just like Dax Davenport, the woman was up to something, and he intended to figure out what."*

# Chapter Eight

&

"WHY DON'T YOU TAKE THE rest of the night off, Dirk? You look done in. Bella and I can handle the last few customers."

Dirk glanced over at the Sanders sisters. They were a year apart in age, but looked more like twins. They were big, dark-haired women with generous figures and even more generous personalities. Just not to each other.

"You mean I can handle the customers," Stella said. "You are slower than Methuselah in the kitchen."

Bella's eyes narrowed as she glared at her sister. "And you rush through the orders so quickly you screw them up half the time. You've had three orders sent back while I've had none."

"At least my food wasn't stone cold by the time it got to the table!"

"No, it was just wrong!"

"Ladies," Dirk held up his hands, "there's no cause for a ruckus. You've both been doing a bang-up job helping me in the kitchen." He winked at Bella. "You are detail-oriented." He winked at Stella. "And you are punctual. As far as I'm concerned, those are both good traits to have."

They smiled broadly, but it was Stella who socked him in the arm so hard that he cringed in pain. "Don't you be using that sweet Texas charm on us, lover boy. Now do what my sister says and go on home. We'll finish up here."

Since there was something he needed to take care of, he took the sisters up on their offer. "Be sure to shut off the lights and lock up. I'll see you both bright and early in the morning." He took off his apron and hung it on a hook before he snagged the last one of Ms. Marble's brownies off a plate.

Bella laughed. "I don't know how you stay so skinny with that sweet tooth of yours." She patted her big belly. "Take my word for it, one day all that sugar will catch up with you."

He figured she was right. One day, everything would catch up with him. But for now, he was still trying to outrun it. When he got in Carly's car, he didn't head toward the motor lodge. He headed toward Becky and Mason's house.

He had been to the house twice in the last few months. Once when Mason was there, and once when he wasn't. The last time, he hadn't found what he was looking for. But seeing the house on Gracie's list had made him wonder if he'd over-looked something. It was possible, given that Ms. Marble had shown up and cut short his search. He wouldn't have to worry about being interrupted tonight. Mason and Becky were in Austin. And Ms. Marble didn't like to be out after dark.

When he arrived, he parked in front of the saggy porch, and then walked around to the side bed-room window he'd used before to enter the house. A light shone through the curtains, but he figured it had been left on for security. It wasn't until he'd slid up the window and slung a leg over the sill that he realized he was wrong. Becky and Mason didn't need to fool people with a light when they had a security system. He'd briefly worked for an alarm company when he was in college and recognized the sensor on the window ledge immediately.

"Shit!" He started to climb back out when a familiar voice stopped him.

"It does appear that you're in a whole heap of that."

He shoved the curtains out of his way. Gracie sat on the floor in the corner of the bedroom. She held a stack of papers in her hands. But he wasn't as interested in the papers as he was in the small leather-bound book that sat on the floor next to her.

He pulled his other leg over the sill and pushed back his cowboy hat. "Howdy, Miss Gracie." He expected her usual blush. Instead, he got a hard, flinty glare that took him back. Obviously, his ploy to end her crush had worked.

"Do you want to explain why you're breaking into Mason and Becky's house?" she asked.

He quickly thought up an excuse. "Mason asked me to stop by and check on things. When I saw the light, I thought there might be an intruder."

He nodded at the stack of papers. "But it looks like it's just a fortune hunter. Another chapter of Tender Heart?"

She looked down at the pages and spoke in a reverent whisper. "Chapter Four."

A true fan of the series would've been ecstatic. Dirk couldn't have cared less. He'd never read the books, and he didn't intend to. He didn't like fiction. He preferred real life stories about real life people. His gaze went to the diary on the floor for a brief second before he returned it to Gracie.

"Congratulations," he said. "What does that make? Five chapters found now?"

She nodded. "Only twenty more to go."

"How do you know there's twenty-five chapters?"

"All her other books have twenty-five chapters. It makes sense that this one would be the same." She glanced up. "If Mason asked you to check on things, why didn't he give you a key to the front door and the security code?"

It was a damned good question. One he didn't have the answer for. Fortunately, he had another excuse in his pocket. He pulled out the paper she'd dropped earlier. "You caught me red handed. I came looking for Tender Heart just like you did."

Her eyes widened. "You stole that from my purse!"

"Now steal is a pretty harsh word, Miss Gracie. I found it on the ground after you left."

"After you and Winnie . . . snuggled?" Her pretty turquoise eyes snapped with fire. "Is that why you're growing the scruff? You need to hide another Winnie mark?"

He stood and rubbed his jaw. "Actually, my razor's dull and I've just been too busy to buy a new one."

"But not too busy to break and enter."

He grinned. "After finding the other two chapters, Tender Heart has become somewhat of an obsession."

She looked more than a little surprised. "You found two chapters? Emery didn't tell me that."

"One in the cemetery and one in the bunkhouse." And ironically, he hadn't been looking for either one.

Gracie carefully put the pages back in the manila envelope. "You shouldn't be wasting your time looking for the book. It belongs to the Arringtons."

He had to wonder if she included herself with the Arringtons. He doubted it. She probably wouldn't take a dime of the money even if she found the rest of the book. Gracie wasn't greedy or money hungry. And she idolized the Arringtons as much as she'd once idolized him.

He nodded at the envelope. "Did you read it?"

She shook her head. "I don't want to read it until all the chapters are found. The only chapter I've read is the first chapter. I had to in order to—" She cut off, and her cheeks turned a rosy red. She was obviously hiding something. And he couldn't help wondering what. She reached for her walker and started to get to her feet, and he hurried over to help her.

"I don't need your help," she snapped.

He took a step back, but remained close enough to help her if she needed it. "I heard that Cole decided to go with Emery to Atlanta. You doing okay at the house by yourself?" Dirk had been more than a little annoyed when he heard about Cole leaving Gracie all alone.

"I'm not a two-year-old who needs a babysitter."

His gaze lowered to the t-shirt that hugged her full breasts. She sure as hell wasn't a two-year-old. "No, but you just got over a serious injury so if you need some help, all you have to do is call." If Cole had wanted Dirk to stay away from her, then he shouldn't have left her without someone to watch over her.

Gracie didn't seem thrilled with the offer. "Thank you, but I'm doing just fine. Now you need to leave so I can lock up."

Since he didn't have much choice, he nodded his head. "I guess I'll just head out the way I came." He walked to the window, pushed back the curtains, and slung a leg over the sill. She followed him, making sure to slam closed the window and lock it once he jumped to the ground. He waited a few seconds before he peeked in through the crack in the curtains.

Gracie moved back to the corner where she knelt on the floor and removed a loose floorboard. The same loose floorboard Dirk had found when he'd searched the house the first time. That time, all he'd found between the joists was the empty box Gracie pulled out. There had been no diary in it when he'd looked. He watched her place the diary in the box, and then place the box back in the floor. Now all he needed to figure out was the security code.

He was so busy thinking about how to get the code that he tripped over a coiled up garden hose. He caught himself before he fell, but it gave him an idea. He yelped as loudly as he could before he sprawled face first on the ground. As he'd hoped, the window opened and Gracie leaned out.

"Dirk?"

He sat up, then scooted over so he was in the light from the window. He brushed at the dirt and grass on his shirt. "Nothing to worry about. I just tripped over the garden hose."

"Are you okay?"

"Right as rain." He got to his feet, then cringed and hobbled. "Well, maybe not that right." As he figured, Gracie's kind heart caved.

"Did you break something? Stay right there. I'll call an ambulance."

He held up a hand. "No need for that. I think I just twisted my ankle. I'll head on home and ice it."

"No, you won't. If it's sprained, we need to ice it right now. Can you make it into the house?"

"I think so, but I probably should come in the door."

She nodded. "I'll meet you." He waited for the curtains to close before he hustled around to the front. Probably a little too fast. She seemed surprised when she opened the door and saw him standing on one leg.

"Here," she turned her walker to him, "use this and go lie down on the bed while I get some ice." Before he could decline, she held onto the wall and moved toward the kitchen.

He felt like the biggest asshole ever. But if he wanted the diary, he didn't have time to feel guilty. He made sure Gracie was in the kitchen before he grabbed up the walker and hurried to the bedroom. It didn't take him long to get the diary out of the floor and tuck it into the waistband of his jeans beneath his shirt. He had just replaced the floorboard and hopped on the bed when Gracie walked in.

She moved a lot better than he thought she would without the walker. She used the wall and then the footboard of the bed for balance, but it didn't look like she needed to. She held out a plastic baggie of ice and looked at his foot. "How are we going to get your boot off? Should we cut it?"

Cut his twelve-hundred-dollar Lucchese boots that he just got worn in? Not likely. Even if he did deserve it. "I'm sure it's not hurt that badly." He sat up and wiggled his foot. "In fact, it's feeling better already. I must've just popped it out of place."

Gracie sent him a suspicious look, but he ignored it and gingerly got to his feet. "Yep, much better." He took the baggie of ice. "I'll just ice this at the motor lodge and let you get back to the ranch." A thought struck him. "Where did you park, anyway? I didn't see your car when I pulled up."

"Your car, not mine. And I parked around back."

His eyebrows lifted. "Are you sure you had permission to be here, Miss Gracie?"

"More than you did, Mr. Hadley."

He laughed. He liked shy Gracie, but he had to admit that he liked this sassy side of her better. It didn't make him feel quite as guilty. He picked up the envelope off the nightstand. "Come on, I'll walk you out."

She didn't look happy about him holding her precious Tender Heart chapter, but she didn't complain. She made him turn his back while she entered the security code and refused his help down the porch steps. On the way to her car, he tried to make small talk. But she wasn't much in the talking mood. He'd really done a number on her with Winnie. He should feel happy that she wasn't infatuated with him anymore, but he just felt kind of empty. Like he'd lost a good friend.

When they reached her car, she refused his help and put her walker in the backseat herself.

"Goodnight, Dirk."

He pulled open her car door and held on to it like a jilted boyfriend who was reluctant to let her go. "Goodnight, Miss Gracie. You drive safe, you hear. And if you should need any help—not you, but with the horses, you let me know. Although I figure Zane sent someone over for that."

She turned to him. In the moonlight, her eyes looked like two reflective pools of turquoise that a man would be more than happy to drown in. They also looked confused.

"Didn't your daddy tell you he was helping with Cole's horses?"

*"Daisy thought it would be so easy to slip out of town unnoticed. But now that she'd caught the eye of Johnny Earhart, she couldn't go anywhere without the annoying man showing up."*

# CHAPTER NINE

(

SOMETHING STARTLED GRACIE FROM A sound sleep. She blinked awake and rolled to her back. Her room had changed very little over the years. The horse print curtains she'd made in her junior high sewing class still hung over her window. The bulletin board was still covered with her barrel-racing ribbons. Her dresser still held high school memorabilia and barrel-racing trophies. And the shelves over her dresser were still filled with stuffed animals, her collection of plastic horses, and a set of the Tender Heart books.

She should've redecorated years ago, or at least before she left for college, but Gracie had never liked change. She took comfort in coming back to find everything the same. But now as she looked around her room, it didn't feel comfortable as much as pathetic. While most women her age were living on their own, she was living in her childhood bedroom surrounded by her childhood things.

She sat up, and her gaze got caught by the stacks of aged paper on her desk. After coming home from Becky and Mason's the night before, she'd pulled out the first chapter of the Tender Heart novel she'd found in the chapel and compared it to the fourth. It was the same paper, and the funky t's and p's proved that Lucy's typewriter had been used to write it. Emery would have to verify it, but Gracie was sure it was authentic.

She got up to take another look at the chapter when shouting drifted in through her open window. She quickly headed for the front door. When she reached the porch, she realized two things: She'd forgotten her walker. And she only wore her nightshirt.

She started to turn back to the house when Holt Hadley came flying out of the barn and landed in the dirt. Dirk followed. He was hatless, and his face held an anger that she'd never seen. The night before, she'd realized that Dirk wasn't happy about his dad taking care of Cole's horses. But she hadn't thought he'd show up and cause trouble. That wasn't Dirk. He was a smiling, easygoing cowboy. He wasn't this snarling hothead.

He grabbed Holt by the front of the shirt and jerked him up from the ground. "Don't you ever talk about her like that again." He shook Holt like a rag doll. "Do you hear me, old man?"

Holt didn't look all that scared. In fact, his cigarette still dangled from his mouth and bobbed as he spoke. "Just stating the truth, son. But if you got the hots for her, I'll wait my turn—"

The punch that Dirk threw sent both the cigarette and Holt flying.

"Dirk!" Gracie moved as quickly as she could down the porch steps and across the yard. She knelt down next to Holt. He was out cold. She looked up at Dirk. "What has gotten into you? He's your father."

"No, he's not. He's just a sperm donor." He walked over and stomped out the cigarette. "You have to care to be a father."

She should understand the statement. Her mother hadn't cared enough to contact Gracie once since deserting her. But Gracie still thought of Ava as her mother, and she couldn't release the silly notion that her mother had a good reason for not contacting her.

Once Holt started coming to, she got to her feet and turned to Dirk. "What are you doing here?"

His gaze sizzled down her body before moving to his father, who was just sitting up. "Getting rid of the riffraff."

She had already decided to fire Holt after his inappropriate comments the day before, and she didn't like Dirk trying to take charge. "You can't just waltz onto the Arrington Ranch and start firing people."

"I'm not firing him. I'm just convincing him that it's time to move on." He reached down and pulled Holt to his feet.

Holt tested his jaw, and then grinned as if he hadn't just been knocked out by Dirk. "You pack quite a punch, son." He looked over at Gracie and winked. "He must've gotten that from his mama's side. My side of the family are more lovers than fighters." He gave her a thorough onceover that had Gracie crossing her arms over her breasts.

"Why you, slimy son of—" Dirk went to grab his father, but Gracie stopped him.

"Enough!" She couldn't remember the last time she'd yelled. Ever since the accident, she'd felt too helpless and weak. It felt good, and even better when Dirk looked so shocked. "Let your father go, Dirk."

When he did, Holt brushed at his shirt. "That's right, son. You listen to the little lady."

She turned on him. "I warned you about smoking in the barn. You're fired."

Holt studied her for a moment before he picked up his cowboy hat and slapped it against his leg. "Now I don't think that's a good idea, ma'am. You need someone to take care of them horses."

"I'll take care of them," Dirk said. "I want you gone from Bliss today."

Holt's eyes twinkled as he pulled on his hat. "Of course, son. I always hate to overstay my welcome." He tipped his hat at Gracie, then whistled as he walked to his truck.

Once he was gone, Dirk visibly relaxed, but his easygoing smile didn't return.

As she studied his serious face, she realized that she didn't know Dirk as well as she thought she did. In fact, she was starting to wonder if she knew him at all. She had shared everything about her life with him, but now she realized that he'd never shared anything with her. Besides the long list of jobs he'd had, she knew nothing about him. She didn't know anything about his family, his history, his thoughts and desires. And how could she possibly have fallen in love with him if she didn't know anything about him? The answer was simple. She'd fallen in love with a fantasy. A fantasy of a handsome, charming cowboy who reminded her of Johnny Earhart in the Tender Heart series. Dirk wasn't Johnny. She didn't know who he was.

He released his breath and ran a hand over his jaw. His scruff was turning into a beard, and his eyes were bloodshot, like he wasn't getting enough sleep. No doubt from all the snuggling he was doing with Winnie.

"I'm sorry," he said. "I didn't mean to put you in the middle of a family fight." He watched the dust settle from Holt's truck. "But he's bad business, Miss Gracie. And I won't have him here stirring up trouble for you."

"He hasn't been causing trouble. You were the one doing that. And stop calling me Miss Gracie. I'm not your maiden aunt."

His gaze lowered to her breasts before it returned to her face. "No. No, you're not."

She couldn't help the blush that heated her cheeks, but she could stop being a spineless twit. "I don't need your help. I'll call Zane. He's not leaving for the wedding until tomorrow, and he can send someone else. Or I'll do it." But just the thought of being near a horse made her muscles tighten in panic. A searing pain shot through her left leg. She gasped and grabbed her thigh.

Dirk moved closer. "What is it?"

"A cramp," she spoke between her clenched teeth.

Without a word, he swept her up in his arms and carried her into the house. She was in too much pain to argue. She couldn't even direct him to her bedroom. But he easily found it, and she had to wonder if the childish décor was a dead giveaway.

He placed her on the bed and took her bare foot in his hand. "Just try to relax," he said. "If we can get you stretched out, it should go away." He climbed onto the bed with her, straddling her one leg so he could hold the cramping one straight up. She had little doubt that her panties were showing, but she was in too much agony to care. She bit her bottom lip to keep from crying out, but a whimper still escaped.

"It's okay, baby," Dirk said as he adjusted her foot in his hand and gently pushed her leg toward her head. "Just remember to breathe." She followed his directions, breathing in and then slowly releasing it. The pain began to recede. After a few moments, she released a long sigh and relaxed on her pillows.

"Better?" Dirk asked.

She nodded, but refused to look at him. Just when she had started to feel strong and in control, her body betrayed her. It was frustrating and maddening. Especially in front of Dirk, who probably did view her as a baby who needed to be coddled.

He leaned into the stretch a few seconds more before he lowered her leg and started massaging her thigh muscles. He talked while his thumbs and fingers kneaded. "Did I ever mention that I once worked as a massage therapist? The key to a great massage is good communication. If it hurts, let me know."

It didn't hurt. It felt heavenly. Or at least it did until his fingers moved up her thigh and the side of his hand brushed the spot between her legs. Then it didn't feel heavenly as much as sinful. Extremely sinful. Her entire body lit up like he'd just flipped on a switch. She was no longer relaxed. Her eyes opened as her muscles tensed for the next touch.

It came only a second later like a stroke from a heated paintbrush. Her gaze snapped down to his hand. Her nightshirt had wiggled up and her panties were showing. The sight of Dirk's long, tanned fingers on the pale skin of her thigh made everything inside her melt like wax under a flame. She closed her eyes and tried to concentrate on something else. But the next brush of his hand caused her concentration to evaporate, and she couldn't hold back her moan.

"Feel good?" he asked.

Oh, it felt good. So good that she wanted more. And when the next faint brush came, she couldn't help lifting her hips to follow his hand. The massage stopped. She opened her eyes to find Dirk frozen with his gaze pinned on her panties. Time seemed to tick by in slow motion as she waited for his long lashes to lift. When they finally did, she expected to see shock. Instead, she saw heat. The same heat that rolled in waves through her.

His lips parted, and he said one word. "Gracie."

She didn't know if he came to her or she went to him. She stopped thinking as soon as their lips met. It was nothing like the kiss she'd given him in the chapel. That had been warm and sweet. This was hot and hungry. That was a one-sided taste. This was a mutual feasting.

Their lips slid and their tongues delved like they couldn't get enough. She lifted her hands and cradled his stubbled jaw, and he shifted to her side, his hand skating under her shirt and palming her breast. He squeezed and released a low, satisfied "ahhh" that vibrated through his tongue to hers. She turned toward him and wrapped her leg around his waist, rubbing her throbbing center against the hard bulge beneath the fly of his zipper. A growl came from deep in the back of his throat. But before it even finished, he pulled away and got off the bed.

He kept his back to her and ran a hand through his hair. "Sorry. I don't know what happened."

She wanted to echo his words. What had happened? Had she almost had sex with Dirk? After she'd decided that she didn't even know him? After he had chosen Winnie over her?

She shoved down her nightshirt and sat up, her voice shaking as she spoke. "I want you to leave."

He placed his hands on her desk, letting his head fall forward as he released a long breath. "Gracie, I—" He cut off when his attention got caught by something on the desk. He reached out and picked up the top piece of paper from the chapter. He turned and showed it to her. "What's this?"

Her voice was cool as she stood and took the page from him. "If you have two chapters, you should recognize a page from the last Tender Heart book." She glanced at the paper. "Although this is just the dedication—" Before she could finish, Dirk turned and walked out, slamming the door behind him.

She stood there stunned for a second before anger sizzled. How dare he kiss her and then just walk out like nothing had happened. She dropped the dedication page to the desk, grabbed a barrel-racing trophy, and chucked it with all her might at the door. It hit with a satisfying thunk, then clattered to the floor. The top broke off and rolled toward her, landing at her bare feet.

The sight of the gold-embossed horse and rider lying on its side triggered something in Gracie's memory. Suddenly, she remembered everything about the accident. The headlights of Cole's truck flashing around the curve. Brandy's tensing muscles before she squealed and threw Gracie. She remembered flying through the air and the mind-numbing pain when she landed. She remembered Cole hysterically clutching her hand and telling her everything was going to be okay as he called the paramedics. She remembered the female paramedic calmly asking if she could move her legs. And she remembered being terrified when she couldn't.

But her fear hadn't been about never walking again. Her fear had been about never riding again. Barrel racing was her life. It was the one thing she'd been successful at. The one thing that made her feel worthy of the Arrington name. Without it, she was nothing.

She looked around her room at all the ribbons and trophies and realized that Calvin was right. She *was* hiding behind her walker. Hiding so she wouldn't have to face the truth that her life had changed. That no matter how hard she'd tried to keep everything the same, everything was different. The only father she ever knew was gone. Cole had fallen in love and gotten married. Becky was starting a new life with Mason. Gracie was the only one who couldn't seem to move forward.

She glanced at her walker sitting next to the bed.

But did she have the strength to release her crutch and face life standing on her own two feet?

*"Johnny hadn't been able to figure out why Dax was in town. But he had figured out what Daisy was up to. She had no intention of being a mail-order bride. She had used the stagecoach ticket his brother had sent and planned on skipping town. And he wasn't going to let her get away with it."*

# CHAPTER TEN

(

TO BONNIE BLUE.
Dirk drove away from the Arrington Ranch with the words he'd read on the dedication page circling around in his head like buzzards over road kill. It changed nothing, and yet it changed everything. He was still the youngest child of Holt and Dotty Hadley. A rascally, willful boy spoiled by his grandma, mama, and three older sisters. A punky adolescent trying to get over his mama's death. A neglected teenager stuck with a deadbeat of a father. A determined college student striving to be top of his class. A ruthless businessman wanting to prove that he wasn't too young to succeed. A sly drifter who deceived an entire town.

But now he was also the great-grandson of Lucy Arrington.

Zane, Cole, and Becky weren't just friends, they were also his cousins. Technically, even Gracie was his cousin. Not by blood, but somehow he didn't think it would make a difference to Gracie. She wanted to be an Arrington so damned badly it wasn't funny. While he didn't want to be an Arrington at all.

And yet, he was.

He pulled over to the side of the road and tried to let everything sink in. He'd never had much of a heritage. His grandfather and grandmother on his mother's side had been raised in an orphanage. And his father's side was a succession of lazy, irresponsible men who would rather sit on their asses and drink beer than keep a decent job, and the sad, disillusioned women who fell in love with them.

His mother had been one of those women. She'd loved Holt with a passion, which was how she'd ended up getting pregnant with triplets at sixteen. They'd gotten married, but Holt was never a husband or father. He would leave for months at a time without sending home a dime to take care of his wife and three daughters. But Dirk's mom would always welcome Holt home with open arms, which was how Dirk had been conceived. Her mother, Granny Bon, called her all kinds of a fool, but his mother said she couldn't resist Holt's smile.

Dirk hated the smile. He'd tried to wipe it right off his father's face this morning when he'd made the comment about Gracie. "I never thought I'd take a cripple to bed, but that pretty little piece of tail—" That was all he'd gotten out before Dirk hit him. He might've beaten him to death if Gracie hadn't stopped him.

Gracie.

He ran a hand over his face and blew out his breath. Why did he have to kiss her? He knew the answer. It was her eyes. The innocence mixed with all that heat had done him in. She hadn't just wanted him. She'd needed him. And he'd needed her too. He needed her to fill him with her innocence, the innocence he'd had taken away when his mother died and his father left, leaving him to be the only man to take care of his grandma and sisters.

Not that his grandmother needed taking care of. She was one tough woman. Still, he'd felt the weight of being the only man in the family. And he hadn't taken the pressure well. He'd become belligerent and started hanging out with a tough crowd. Dirk had only gone for a joyride in a stolen car twice before he was caught. Having his grandmother show up at the detention center with his father and a look of disappointment in her eyes had been enough to cure him of ever stealing again. Even after going to live with his father, he'd kept that vow. But he had lied. He'd lied about his age to get jobs. And now he was lying about who he was to help his grandmother.

He pulled out his cellphone and glanced at the time. His grandmother would already be at work. At sixty-five, she should be retired, but Bonnie Blue Davidson had always been a hardworking, sassy woman who didn't believe in sitting around and twiddling her thumbs.

"It's about time you called, Dirky," she said as soon as she answered the phone.

The nickname never failed to make him cringe. "Sorry, Granny Bon, I've been a little busy doing your bidding."

"I didn't ask you to stay in that town for all these months. I just asked you to find out the truth."

"The truth doesn't always come easy. Especially when you don't want anyone to know you're looking for it. It would've been much easier if you'd let me tell people what I was looking for."

She released her breath in a huff. "You couldn't just waltz into that town and say your grandmother thinks she might be Lucy Arrington's illegitimate daughter. This is Texas, where people shoot first and ask questions later. Especially diehard Tender Heart fans."

He couldn't deny that. The fans he'd met were pretty rabid about the series. "And you don't think they'll shoot me if they find out I've been lying to them for all these months?"

There was a long pause before she spoke. "You're right." It was easy to hear the disappointment in her voice. "It's time for you to leave Bliss. If you haven't found any proof by now, I doubt that you will. And I shouldn't have asked you for this favor in the first place. I guess I just wanted to know who my real mama was, and when that man showed up with that birth certificate, I thought I'd found her."

When Granny Bon first told Dirk about the man who had come to her house, he was more concerned about his grandmother letting a stranger into her home and serving him sweet tea than the birth certificate she was jabbering about. After living with Holt for years, Dirk didn't trust anyone, especially a man who hadn't given Granny Bon his

name. All the man had was a copy of a birth certificate with Lucy Arrington's name as the mother
and Bonnie Blue as the child. There had been no
father's name.

Dirk thought it was a hoax thought up by someone who knew how well Dirk's business was going
and was running some kind of scam. But Granny
Bon had been convinced that there was some truth
in the man's claims.  And after all his grandmother
had been through, Dirk couldn't deny her.

His grandmother's story was sadder than Gracie's. Instead of leaving her with a loving family,
Bonnie Blue's mother had left her at an orphanage. That would've turned out okay if she'd been
adopted. But Bonnie Blue had been a sickly child
and hadn't left the orphanage until she was sixteen.
Not only had she survived living in an orphanage,
but she'd also survived the early death of her husband, her only daughter dying in a car accident,
and years of raising four grandkids all by herself.
He owed her more than just a few months out of
his life. He owed her everything.

Which was why he'd come to Bliss in search of
the truth. After all these months, he was happy he
finally had something for her. Even if it left him
feeling completely blindsided.

"I found proof."

He could almost see her gray eyes snapping with
excitement. "What kind of proof? Did you finally
get your hands on Lucy's diary? Did she mention
getting pregnant? Did she mention me?"

Dirk had stayed up all night long reading Lucy's
diary. He now knew that she wasn't the old maid
everyone thought she was. She'd had a torrid love

affair with someone she called Honey Bee. But talking sex with his grandmother wasn't something he was wiling to do. So he only told her the highlights.

"I read the diary, and Lucy did have a lover. But she didn't mention who he was or anything about getting pregnant."

"Then what's your proof?"

"I saw the first chapter of the final Tender Heart book. She dedicated it to Bonnie Blue."

There was a long stretch of silence before his grandmother spoke. It was easy to hear the tears in her voice. "She dedicated her final book to me."

It wasn't a question. It was a reverent statement of awe. Like Lucy had given her some special gift. At that moment, Dirk had never hated anyone as much as he hated Lucy Arrington. What kind of a coldhearted bitch would drop her kid off at an orphanage and then try to alleviate her guilt by dedicating a book to her? If Lucy had wanted to give his grandmother something, she should've given her a mother. But he couldn't point that out. Not when his grandma was so happy.

"They told me that my mama gave me my name, but I didn't believe it until now," she said. "I used to dream about my mama being some famous person, but I never thought she'd turn out to be someone so important."

"She was only a writer, Granny Bon. It isn't like she discovered penicillin."

His grandmother was like Gracie, you couldn't say one bad word about Lucy Arrington to her without getting your head bit off. "Now, don't you be so cold-hearted. There are lots of reasons for the choices people make in life, and you shouldn't judge unless you've walked in their shoes."

He rolled his eyes. "Fine. Now the question is what do you want to do about this information? Lucy didn't leave a cent to her family so you'll get nothing there."

He didn't know why he brought up money. He knew his grandmother couldn't care less about it. She still hadn't spent a dime of the money he'd given her. Maybe he just wanted to point out another one of Lucy's flaws. Which was a shitty thing to do, and his grandmother didn't let him get away with it.

"The biggest mistake I made was not fighting that judge harder when he gave your father custody over you. The three years you spent with that snake has you confused about what's important in life. And it sure as heck isn't a big bank account. I care nothing about Lucy's money. That's not why I sent you to Bliss. Nor did I send you to cause a ruckus. I wanted to know who my mama was. That's all. Now that I know, that's enough for me."

"You don't want to meet the Arringtons?"

"If Lucy had wanted her family to know about me, I figure she would've told them. And as popular as she was, I understand why she didn't. I would hate to drag her name through the gutter just because I want to meet a few relatives. Now you need to quit worrying about me and get back to your life."

It was strange. When he first came to Bliss, he couldn't wait to prove that the birth certificate the man had shown his grandmother was false and get back to Dallas and his company. But now that his time in Bliss was up, he wasn't all that excited about getting back to his life. Running a successful company didn't hold the same interest for him. Neither did his new house in Dallas. Or the European vacation he'd planned. Which made him realize how attached he'd become to the town.

He might not care anything about the Tender Heart series or Lucy, but he had come to care about the people of Bliss. They were hardworking folks with high morals and big hearts. They had welcomed him with open arms, treating him like a member of their community and a trusted friend.

He enjoyed playing dominos with Emmett at the gas station, swapping stories with Hank, the owner of the Watering Hole, and doing odd jobs for Ms. Marble. But he especially enjoyed being with the Arringtons, and he counted them as his friends. They'd been through a lot in the last year. Cole and Gracie losing their father. Zane getting a divorce from his first wife. Becky losing the ranch she'd dreamed about owning. But all three had gotten through those tough times and found love.

Dirk had been a witness. He'd watched them fall head over heels and been in every one of their weddings. A part of him was proud to call them his friends. The other part felt guilty as hell for deceiving them. And he hated that he'd have to leave without coming clean. But Granny Bon was right. With as much as they looked up to their great-aunt, he couldn't see them being overjoyed that she'd had an illegitimate child. It was best to leave Lucy Arrington up on her pedestal.

"Okay, Granny Bon," he said. "If that's the way you want it, we'll keep our little secret. As soon as

Carly gets back from Atlanta, I'll head out. Spring has been bugging me to come to Houston for a few weeks before I go to Europe."

"All three of the girls have been bugging me to come visit. I don't think they're as happy as they thought they would be living in a big city. Once a country girl, always a country girl." The sound of squealing, laughing children drifted through the receiver. "I need to go and give the kids something to keep them busy."

His grandmother had worked in a doctor's office for years as a clerical assistant. Now she ran a transitional home for kids who had been taken from their parents due to abuse and neglect. Those kids couldn't have asked for a more loving woman to heal their wounds.

"I love you, Granny Bon," he said.

"I love you too, Dirky." She paused. "And I thank you for giving me a mama."

Dirk was not a crier, but damned if his eyes didn't well up with tears. "You're welcome." He hung up and sat there for a moment, trying to digest everything: Lucy being his great-grandmother. The Arringtons being his cousins. Leaving Bliss. But especially leaving Gracie.

She was the only one who hadn't found her happily-ever-after. And damned if he didn't want to stick around for that. Of all the Arringtons, she was the one who had been through the most. She deserved some happiness. Of course, him sticking around wouldn't help with that. He had thought that faking a relationship with Winnie had made Gracie hate him. But there was no hate in the kiss they'd shared. Just heat. A whole helluva lot of heat.

The second he'd lifted his gaze from her panties and looked in her smoldering eyes, he'd been toast. He couldn't even remember moving. All he could remember was the hot slide of her lips and the scorching brush of her tongue. He'd been with his fair share of women and had some damn hot sex, but that kiss was the most mind-blowing sensual experience of his life. And he'd never forget it. Or the woman who gave it to him.

The sound of a truck coming up the road pulled his attention away from his thoughts. He recognized the black pickup heading toward him immediately. He was glad Zane was coming to check on Gracie. He felt bad about leaving her without a word. He waited until Zane pulled along side him before he rolled down the window. He studied Zane's features carefully, but could find no resemblance between him and his cousin.

"Car trouble?" Zane asked. "I've been after Carly to get a new car ever since we got married, but she thinks a Subaru is the best car ever made. Just shows you what city girls know."

"You're damn straight there, Boss." Dirk had gotten in a habit of calling Zane boss when he worked for him. Some habits were hard to break. "I bottom out every time I go over fifteen on these back roads. But the engine seems to run pretty well." He held up his cellphone. "I just stopped to make a phone call."

Zane lifted an eyebrow. "Yeah, I guess around here, you need to worry about getting in an accident—especially during rush-hour traffic."

Dirk laughed. "Better safe than sorry. So how are you holding up without Carly cooking for you?"

"Not well. Cheese sandwiches and omelets are about the extent of my culinary expertise."

"Pot roast is on the menu tonight at the diner. Or as Carly refers to it, braised beef. If you stop by, I'll give you the friends and family discount."

"Friends and family? I own the damn diner."

"But you're not my boss anymore, Boss. And I have strict orders from Carly that nothing but water and coffee are on the house."

Zane's cellphone rang. He glanced at the screen on his dashboard. "Speak of the devil." He tapped the screen. "No need to get worried, Carly Sue. I promised I'd be there in time for the wedding and I'll—" He cut off when faint sobbing came through the speakers. Dirk had never seen a man's face go so deathly pale in his life, and Dirk was just as concerned. Carly wasn't the type of woman who cried over nothing.

"What is it, honey?" Zane asked. "Did you get in an accident? Are you hurt?" His hands tightened on the steering wheel. "Do I need to kick someone's ass?"

"Yes." Carly said over the crying that obviously wasn't hers. "Savannah's fiancé's. He just called off the wedding."

*"The mail-order brides weren't as annoying as Daisy first thought. Valentine Clemens told funny stories about her time spent as a saloon girl. Laura Thatcher was an amazing cook. And Etta Jenkins gave Daisy a diary to record her adventures in."*

# CHAPTER ELEVEN

❧

IT WAS HARD TO SLEEP with sobs coming through the wall. Gracie sat up and glanced at the clock. Savannah had been crying now for close to two hours. Of course, according to Emery and Cole, she'd been sobbing off and on the entire trip back to Bliss. And Gracie couldn't blame her. What kind of a man broke up with you three days before your wedding?

Gracie wasn't as close to Savannah as she was to Emery and Carly. Not only because Savannah lived in Atlanta, but also because they didn't have anything in common. Savannah was a southern belle who dressed in designer clothes and always wore high heels and perfect makeup. Gracie was a country girl who was more comfortable in boots and a little lip gloss.

That, and she thought Savannah was kind of

ditzy.

But, ditzy or not, Gracie still couldn't let her keep crying without offering some kind of comfort. When she'd been upset as a kid, Cole had always made her a cup of hot cocoa. And even though it was late August and hotter than heck, Gracie went into the kitchen to make a cup.

She'd stopped using her walker. Calvin was right. She was strong enough to walk without it. But she still felt unsteady. Not her body as much as her mind. Now that she'd finally accepted that she needed to move forward with her life, she didn't know in what direction to go. She felt lost and uncertain. She'd stayed up most of the night thinking about it and still didn't have any answers. In college, she had waffled on her major so much her counselor had finally recommended a degree in university studies. She'd been months away from graduating when she had the accident. But did she want to finish a degree she'd never wanted in the first place? And if she didn't get her degree, what did she want to do?

The only thing she'd truly enjoyed doing in the last six months was forging the Tender Heart chapters. She was surprised at how much she'd loved getting into her characters' minds. And when Emery had told her she had a knack for writing, she'd continued to scribble down stories in her journal. But that was just for fun. She would never be good enough to write a book and get it published. Which left her with no answers at all.

Feeling more than a little depressed, she made two cups of cocoa, added generous squirts of whipped cream, and then carefully carried them to the guestroom. She set one down on the hall table before tapping softly on Savannah's door.

The sobbing stopped, and a second later, Savannah opened the door. Even with puffy eyes and tear-streaked cheeks, she was beautiful. Her hair was a bright red that had been softened with strawberry-blond highlights and auburn lowlights and her eyes were a light blue that bordered on lavender. She wore a white negligee and robe set that seemed a little ridiculous for the ranch, but not as ridiculous as the white Persian cat with the rhinestone collar she clutched in her arms.

Gracie held up the cocoa. "I brought you some hot chocolate."

Savannah sniffed. "Oh, how sweet, Gracie Lynn." She put the cat down to take the cup, and the fluffy animal streaked out the open door like its tail was on fire. "Miss Pitty Pat!" She called in a hushed voice. But the cat disappeared down the hallway.

"Do you want me to go get her?" Gracie asked.

Savannah sighed. "No. She's probably as sick of listening to me cry as everyone else." She smiled weakly and took the cup. "I guess I'm keeping up the entire house with my sniveling. I told Emery I should've gone to the motor lodge. Or just stayed in Atlanta." Tears welled in her eyes. "Of course, I don't have a home there any longer. I certainly can't live with Miles after . . ." She left the word hanging as a sob broke free.

Gracie reached out and gently squeezed her arm. "You can stay here for as long as you need to."

"That's real nice of you, honey." Savannah hiccupped and shook her head forlornly. "I don't know what happened. He never once acted like he was unhappy. Then all of a sudden he shows up and says he doesn't want to get married. Talk about being dumbstruck."

Gracie could sympathize. She was feeling a little dumbstruck herself. Dirk had kissed her. Not a quick friendly peck or even a light boyfriend brush. He'd kissed her as if he couldn't get enough of her. As if he wanted to consume her. If he kissed all women like that, no wonder Winnie was panting after him. Gracie wanted to pant after him too. But she flat refused to become dopey over Dirk again.

"Men are jerks," she said.

"Amen to that." Savannah dabbed at her eyes with the tissue in her hand. "And they certainly aren't worth messing up a good makeup job." She pushed open the door. "Did you want to come in and talk for a little while?" Since it looked like she could use some company, Gracie picked up her cocoa and stepped inside.

The guestroom had a futon couch that folded into a bed against one wall and shelves and shelves of books on the others. Savannah left the door open and climbed back onto the futon with her cup of hot chocolate. Gracie sat down on the opposite end.

"Were all these books Lucy's?" Savannah asked.

"Some of them, but most of them belong to me. I'm a bit of a bookworm."

"This is quite a collection. Are you the one who placed them in alphabetical order by author?"

Gracie blushed. "I had a lot of time on my hands after the accident. Plus, it helps me to keep track when people borrow them."

Savannah looked confused. "People borrow them? Doesn't Bliss have a library?"

"No. I guess we're too small of a town for a library."

Savannah's mouth dropped. "Why, that's just plain crazy. Especially when Lucy donates all her royalties to the Texas library system. And her own town doesn't even get a library?"

It had never made sense to Gracie either. "Joanna Daily, who is head of the town council, has been trying for years to get one, but I guess it has to do with the population."

Miss Pitty Pat came prancing back into the room and jumped on the futon, startling Savannah. "Sweet Baby Jesus!" She held a hand to her abundant breasts. "You scared the heck out of me, Pitty." She picked up the cat and cuddled it. "But I forgive you." She sat back on the futon, placed the cat on her lap, and reached for her cup of hot chocolate. "Now tell me about the man who's been a jerk to you."

Gracie was a little taken back by the request. She'd never talked about her infatuation with Dirk to anyone—not even Becky. But it looked like Savannah desperately needed someone to commiserate with. It had to be tough to be left at the altar when your two best friends had just gotten married and were so happy. And maybe talking about Dirk wouldn't just help Savannah. Maybe it would help Gracie to move on.

She glanced at the door. "I've never told anyone about this, so I would appreciate if you kept it to yourself."

Savannah mimicked zipping her mouth. "My lips

are sealed tighter than a Ziploc bag." She took a sip of her cocoa, leaving a whipped cream mustache on her top lip. "Start from the beginning. I just adore a good love story."

The story came out much easier than Gracie expected. She told Savannah about the first time she'd seen Dirk. About how he'd been standing in the barn and the sunlight from a hole in the roof surrounded him like angelic light from heaven. She told her about how her wheelchair had tipped over and Dirk had helped her up. Instead of making her feel like a complete idiot, he'd told her a funny story about backing into a sheriff's car when he was a teenager.

As she talked about him helping on the ranch in exchange for her car, her eyes filled with tears. "He brought me chickens," she said. "The cutest chickens you've ever seen in your life."

"Animals make the best gifts as far as I'm con-cerned," Savannah said. "Of course, I'm scared of anything bigger than Miss Pitty." She shivered. "And flapping feathers give me the willies. But so far it doesn't sound like Dirk has been that big of a jerk to you. In fact, after your story, I'm half in love with him."

Gracie didn't waste any time telling her about Winnie and the hickey, and finally the kiss he gave her in her bedroom. When she was finished, Savan-nah was reclined back on the bed with her eyes closed and Miss Pitty Pat sleeping on her chest. Gracie thought she'd put her to sleep with the story, but just as she was about to ease off the futon and go back to her room, Savannah's eyes flashed open.

"The entire Winnie thing sounds fishy to me. Dirk never did like Winnie. I just can't see him wanting to go to bed with her."

Gracie stretched out her legs and rubbed her muscles that were getting cramped. "I saw the hickey with my own eyes—or not the hickey as much as the Band-Aid he used to cover it."

"I guess when sex is involved there's no accounting for taste." Savannah stared up at the ceiling and petted the cat. "But at least Dirk didn't make you any promises. At least he didn't take your entire future and wad it up in a little ball and toss it in the trash." Tears leaked out of the corners of her eyes. "I had everything all planned out. Our wedding. Our house. The number of kids we were going to have. Now look at me. I have no life whatsoever."

Gracie leaned back against the wall. "At least you have a career and a way to make money. At least you're not a financial burden to your family."

Savannah lifted her head. "You are not a burden on your family, Gracie Lynn Arrington."

"Yes I am. I should be paying Cole back all the money he's spent on me so he doesn't have to work so hard. If I could just find the rest of the Tender Heart chapters, he'd have plenty of money." She paused and glanced at Savannah. "I found another chapter."

Savannah sat up quickly, rolling the sleeping cat to her lap. "Sweet Baby Jesus! Are you kidding?"

"No. I found it at Mason and Becky's house. I was planning on calling Emery to tell her, but . . ."

"But then I got dumped." Savannah didn't look sad as much as thoughtful. "Why Mason and Becky's house?"

It appeared that Gracie sucked at keeping secrets. Hopefully, Savannah was much better. "You can't tell anyone, but that was where Lucy used to meet her lover."

Savannah's eyes sparkled with contentment. "That's so romantic. I worried about Lucy spending her entire life without someone to love. I'm glad she found someone." She counted off on her fingers. "So that makes five chapters that have been found."

"Five chapters and a lot more to go. Emery and I made a list of possible places, but I've only had a chance to check out Becky's house. I thought I would check out Raff's tomorrow. Although I don't think we'll find one there."

"Raff? Isn't he the mysterious cousin that no one ever sees?"

Gracie laughed. "I don't know if I'd call him mysterious. He's just a loner who does his own thing."

"And why don't you think a chapter will be there?

"Because all the chapters found had something to do with Lucy. And the Tender Heart Ranch didn't exist when Lucy was alive. The barn and house were built after Raff's, Zane's, and Cole's fathers divided the ranch. The only thing on the property at the time Lucy was living was Gus's old cabin and it was vacant."

"Gus? Are you talking about the Gus who started the Arrington cattle dynasty in the late eighteen hundreds?"

"That's him." Miss Pitty Pat got up and stretched, and her large fluffy tail swiped across Gracie's face.

Savannah frowned. "So the cabin has nothing to do with Lucy's stories."

Gracie shook her head. "Gus only lived there until he got married. His bride was the very first mail-order bride—" She paused as her eyes widened. "The mail-order brides. Gus was the one who sent for the brides. He was the one who started it all. Without him, there would be no Tender Heart series."

Savannah bounced up and down with excitement, causing Miss Pitty Pat to send her an annoyed look before jumping to the floor. "Gus's cabin. Another chapter will be in Gus's cabin!"

*"It was hard to keep the smile off his face as he watched Daisy try to kick the nag of a horse into a full gallop. The horse continued to mosey along at a snail's pace that Johnny's horse easily caught up with. 'Goin' for a morning ride, are you?' he asked."*

# CHAPTER TWELVE

C

"YOU'RE QUITTING?" CARLY STARED AT Dirk as if he'd just stabbed her in the back with one of the kitchen knives. "What do you mean you're quitting? You can't quit. You're my assistant manager. My right-hand man." She held up her hands. "Okay, I get it. I've been putting a lot of pressure on you lately by running off for my honeymoon and then Savannah's wedding. But I promise I won't be leaving again. In fact, why don't you take a week off—with pay? And when you get back, we can talk about a raise."

"It's about time you realized my worth, Carly Sue." Dirk tried to tease a smile out of her, but she still looked stunned. He was feeling stunned himself. It was hard coming to terms with the fact that he was an Arrington. It was even harder to explain things to Carly without telling her the truth. "It's not about the money or you leaving me in charge," he said. "I enjoyed running the diner while you were gone."

"Then what is it? Why are you quitting?"

"I'm leaving." He didn't know why it was a struggle to get the words out. He should be happy that his commitment to his grandmother was over. Since coming to Bliss, he'd worked his butt off to get in the good graces of the townsfolk so they'd confide in him. He'd fixed leaky faucets and toilets at the motor lodge, built cabinets for Hank at the Watering Hole bar, pumped gas at Emmett's gas station, baled hay for Zane and Becky, cooked for Carly at the diner, and helped Cole and Gracie clean up their ranch. He should be happy to go back to his easy life of answering emails, sitting in on the occasional conference call, golfing with business connections, and dating models and Dallas Cowboys cheerleaders.

And maybe that was it. Maybe in the last two years life had become too easy. When he first started his tech company with his college buddy Ryker, he'd felt challenged and excited. But now that it was up and running, he just felt bored. He missed working with his hands. He missed dealing with people face to face. He missed feeling like he was part of a community. And there was no deny-ing that he'd become part of Bliss's community. The sad look on Carly's face said it all.

"Leaving? As in leaving for good?"

He nodded and tried to make light of it. "Hey, I'm a drifter. Everyone knows that. And drifters . . . drift." Carly stared at him, and her big brown eyes filled with moisture. "Hey, don't you dare cry on me, Carly Sue. That's why I chose you to tell. You're never been a crier, and I hope you're not going to start now."

She blinked before turning back to the pan of baby back ribs she was rubbing with spices. "Don't be silly. I don't cry. And I certainly wouldn't cry over some cocky cowboy." She paused. "Even if he's become like a little brother to me."

He ignored the tightness in his chest. "Don't you mean big brother?" He ruffled her short, curly hair. "You're the little one."

She socked him in the arm. "I bet you annoy the hell out of your big sisters." She finished rubbing the ribs before she walked to the sink to wash her hands. "I would've liked to meet them. Do they look like you and your father?"

"No," he said. "They look like my mama." And Lucy Arrington. Same coal-black hair and same deep twilight blue eyes. He had been unwilling to admit it before, but he had to admit now. Like it or not, Lucy was his great-grandmother.

She dried her hands and turned. "Well, I bet they have your same personality. You and your father are the life of any party. Holt kept the ranch hands in stitches while he was staying at the ranch. We were sad to see him go." She paused. "Did you have something to do with his leaving? He packed up and left without a word of goodbye."

Obviously, Gracie hadn't mentioned his fight with his father. He was glad. He didn't need to get into that with Carly. "That's my daddy for you. He's not much on goodbyes."

"And I take it you aren't either. Which is why you're sneaking away before the sun comes up."

"Let's just say that I prefer hellos to goodbyes."

She crossed her arms. "Zane is going to be pissed. And Becky will throw a fit when she finds out you left before she could get back from Austin."

"Zane is too busy with the ranch and Becky is too busy with her new husband to worry about an ol' drifter."

She studied him. "I think we both know that you're not a drifter. I don't know who you are, but you're not a drifter."

He wasn't surprised that Carly had figured it out. She wasn't just tough, she was smart. He wanted to tell her the truth, but he couldn't go against his grandmother's wishes. So he didn't say anything.

"Okay," she said. "Keep your secrets, but I hope you're not planning on slinking out of town without saying goodbye to Gracie. I think you owe her a goodbye after leading her on with that kiss."

He stared at her. "Gracie told you?"

"No, Savannah. Gracie confided in the wrong person. Savannah can't keep a secret to save her soul."

Dirk didn't know what to say. He'd spent most of the night thinking about Gracie and the kiss. He didn't know if he wanted to apologize or thank her for giving him such an amazing memory to carry with him. He wanted to say goodbye to her. He also wanted to tell her the truth about Winnie. He couldn't stand the thought of leaving with her hating him. But that was his ego talking. It would be easier on her if he left things the way they were.

He unhooked the backpack from his shoulder and set it on the counter. "Would you make sure Gracie gets this?"

Carly looked at the backpack. "I'm going to make a guess and say inside are the chapters of Lucy's final book that you found."

He nodded. "Tell Gracie . . ." he paused, searching for the right words. "Tell her I hope she finds Tender Heart." He picked up his duffel bag and slung it over his shoulder. "Keep the stove hot and the lemonade cold, Carly Sue." With a wink, he turned and headed for the back door. She stopped him before he reached it.

"Dirk!" He turned in time to catch her as she hugged him tight. "If you ever need anything, I mean anything, you don't hesitate to call."

He swallowed hard and brushed a kiss on the top of her head. "Will do. Now let me go before you crack a rib."

"I'll crack more than a rib if you don't call occasionally to let me know how you are." She drew back, and damned if tears didn't shimmer in her big brown eyes. Before they could fall, he walked out the door.

Once outside, he wasted no time heading down the alley to the street. The sun was just peeking over the horizon, tinting the town in shades of pink. There were still a lot of empty buildings, but with Emery putting the mail-order brides' diaries into a book and Carly opening the diner, people had started taking pride in their town. The businesses that existed had painted and spruced up their storefronts, and the money made from the Fourth of July Chili Cook-off paid for new streetlights that held hanging planters. If they could get other businesses to invest in the town, Dirk could see Bliss surviving and thriving. The town had heart. Maybe that's why Lucy had named her fictional town *Tender Heart*.

He headed down Main Street and kept an eye out for someone he could hitch a ride with. Being that it was so early in the morning, very few cars passed. After he'd hoofed it for a good mile, he wished he'd waited a little longer to leave Bliss. Cowboy boots weren't the most comfortable long-distance walking shoes, especially in the August heat. When he finally heard a car coming up behind him, he turned and stuck out his thumb, praying for a familiar face. But he didn't recognize the vintage pickup. The red and white '67 Chevy was in mint condition, and Dirk couldn't help tipping back his cowboy hat and admiring it as it passed. It only got a little ways down the road before the taillights lit up, and it pulled over to the shoulder.

Dirk jogged to the driver's side just as the window rolled down. The man who leaned out was one mean-looking sonofabitch. He had a scar that ran from his cheekbone to the dark scruff that covered his jaw and chin. His nose looked like it had been broken—not so many times so it was crooked or flat, but just enough to let you know that he didn't have a problem taking a punch. A tattoo of orange and red flames and barbed wire covered his left bicep and disappeared beneath the sleeve of his black t-shirt. His mouth was unsmiling, and his hazel eyes dark and piercing beneath the brim of his cowboy hat.

"Where you headed?" he asked.

"Austin." Dirk stuck a hand out. "Dirk Hadley."

The man hesitated briefly before he reached out the window and took Dirk's hand in a firm grip.

He didn't offer his name. "I'm not going quite that far, but I can get you closer." He tipped his head. "You can sit up front. The back's full."

Dirk jogged around the back, taking note of the groceries and old furniture in the bed of the truck. Once he was in the passenger's seat, he reached for his seatbelt. There was no shoulder strap, just a single belt that went across his lap. It was cool as hell.

"Nice truck," he said. "Is it original?"

The man pulled back on the highway. "Everything but the upholstery."

"You restore it yourself?"

The man nodded, and Dirk made one last ditch effort at conversation. "That's a lot of furniture you got in the back. Are you moving in or out?"

"Neither. I picked it up at an auction in Texarkana."

"You must have a thing for antiques."

"Yep."

Obviously, the man wasn't much of a talker. So Dirk settled back in the seat and decided to keep his mouth shut. They drove in silence for a few miles, and Dirk had started to nod off when the man finally spoke. "It looked like you were coming from Bliss? You live there?"

Dirk blinked awake and rubbed at his eyes. "I worked there for a few months."

The man glanced over. "Do you have family there?"

He paused before he shook his head. "No. I was just passing through and got sidetracked."

The man studied him, which gave Dirk time to study him. From this angle, he couldn't see the scar. Without that distraction, there was something familiar about the man's face.

"Have we met before?" he asked.

The man returned his attention to the road. "Nope." He flipped on his blinker and took the turn that lead to the Arrington ranches.

"You're headed to the Arringtons'?"

There was a slight lift at the corner of his mouth. "You could say that."

Dirk's neck muscles tightened. "Who are you?"

The man glanced at Dirk. "I think the question is what are you doing in Bliss, Mr. Hadley? Or should I call you cuz?"

*"Daisy's Diary entry one: I HATE Johnny Earhart!"*

# CHAPTER THIRTEEN

☙

"**I** THINK WE SHOULD'VE WAITED UNTIL morning to come on our treasure hunt." Savannah nervously glanced out her side window. "It's way too dark and these roads are way too treacherous." She grabbed the dashboard when Gracie's car hit another bump in the road. "I swear I should've worn my athletic bra. My girls are jiggling more than my Aunt Sally's arm fat."

Gracie laughed, something she did often with Savannah. The woman was constantly saying something funny and endearing. Although she worried more than anyone Gracie had ever met.

"Have there ever been any mass murders in Bliss? It would probably be pretty easy to lie in wait for unsuspecting women who are stupid enough to be driving late at night on deserted country roads."

"Not that I know of. But I promise I won't stop for any hitchhikers." As soon as the word came out of Gracie's mouth, an image of Dirk popped into her head. But he wouldn't be standing on the side of the road with his thumb out. He'd never be standing on the side of the road again. Or cooking at the diner. Or chatting with the townsfolk at Emmett's gas station. Or stopping by to talk with Cole.

He was gone.

And it felt like he'd taken a piece of her heart with him.

She'd tried to convince herself that she didn't know enough about him to be in love with him. But now that he was gone, she realized that wasn't true. She knew the important things about Dirk. She knew he was kind, hardworking, and always willing to help a friend. He'd certainly helped her. He'd helped her through one of the most difficult times in her life and convinced her to go to the rehabilitation center. If not for him, she would still be hiding in her wheelchair. She wouldn't be driving down a dirt road in the middle of the night looking for more Tender Heart chapters.

If not for him, she wouldn't have two more chapters in her possession.

*I hope she finds Tender Heart.* The message Dirk left had been stuck in her mind since Carly had dropped off the backpack. He could've just meant he hoped she found the rest of the chapters. But Gracie couldn't help wondering if he meant something more by the message. Something deeper.

"Emery and Carly should've come with us on this mission," Savannah interrupted her thoughts. "There's safety in numbers."

"Then they'd have to explain to Zane and Cole. And Zane and Cole aren't as excited about the last book as we are."

"Or maybe Emery and Carly just didn't want to

leave their warm beds with their hot husbands." Savannah reached into her purse and pulled out a bottle of wine.

"Where did you get that?"

"I bought it today." She wedged the bottle between her legs and took a corkscrew out of her purse. "After our beaux left us, I figured we needed more than a cup of hot cocoa. I would've brought glasses, but I was worried they'd break in my purse."

Gracie steered around another pothole. "Dirk wasn't my beau. He was just a friend who never made any promises."

"Now I don't know about that. You don't kiss a friend like he kissed you. That's called lust. And lust is only a hop, skip, and a jump away from love." Savannah pulled the cork out with a pop.

Lust? It was surprising how much Gracie liked the sound of that. If she couldn't have his love, she should've taken his lust. But it was too late now to get either. Dirk was gone.

"But let's not think about Dirk or Miles tonight." Savannah held up the wine bottle. "To finding the final book of Tender Heart and getting a happily ever after for our favorite characters." She took a deep drink, and then handed it to Gracie.

"To finding Tender Heart," Gracie echoed before taking a drink and handing it back.

Savannah searched through the stations until she landed on country oldies. Ironically, it was Tammy Wynette singing about standing by your man. Savannah and Gracie exchanged looks before they started singing the song at the top of their lungs. A few miles down the road, Savannah suddenly cut off and pointed out the windshield at the barbed wire heart attached to a fencepost.

"What's that?"

"That's the entrance to the Tender Heart Ranch."

Savannah glanced over at her with pure disappointment. "That's it? I thought it would be a big arching entrance sign like Cole and Zane's ranches."

"At one time, there was one. But Raff took it down and replaced it with the barbed wire heart when he took over the ranch."

Savannah continued to look at the rusted heart as they passed. "This Raff is sounding weirder and weirder."

Gracie laughed. "He does march to the beat of a different drummer. But he's a good man. No one knows this, but he came back after my accident and slipped into my hospital room late one night. Unlike Cole and Zane, he didn't try to console me by telling me everything was going to be all right. He just gave me a kiss on the forehead, and then sat down in the chair next to my bed and started reading a book from the Tender Heart series. That gesture meant more to me than all the cards and flowers people sent."

Savannah took anther drink from the wine bottle. "The series does have a way of giving people hope. I never would've made it out of Louisiana if not for that series."

Gracie glanced over at her. "Louisiana? I thought you grew up in Georgia."

Savannah cleared her throat. "Did I say Louisiana?" She placed a hand on her chest. "Lordy, this wine must be stronger than I thought. What I meant was—" She cut off when Gus's cabin came into view. "Sweet Baby Jesus."

Gracie could understand why Savannah was so shocked. Gus's cabin had never been much to look at to begin with, and after months of neglect it was even more pathetic. Waist-high weeds covered the entire yard and the headlights reflected off the silky spider webs that hung in the corners of every window.

"It's a good thing Carly isn't here," Savannah said. "With her fear of spiders, she wouldn't set foot in that house. And I'm not so sure that I want to either."

But Gracie didn't care about the spider webs or even the weeds. She thought the cabin was beautiful. While the roof and windows had been changed numerous times over the years, the original walls of hand-hewn logs still stood. As did the large oak door that had kept out outlaws, Comanches, and Gus when his mail-order bride had been making a point.

Gracie loved the little log cabin as much as she loved everything else that had to do with the Arringtons' history. She drove over the weeds and parked next to the porch steps. She turned off the engine and looked at Savannah, who couldn't seem to take her gaze off the cabin. "If you want to stay in the car, I'm okay with that. Or you could go look in the barn while I'm in the cabin."

Savannah shook her head. "No, I'm more afraid of farm animals than spiders." She guzzled a lot more wine before placing the bottle in the cup holder in the console. "Let's do this."

Despite her brave words, once they were out of the car Savannah wasted no time taking Gracie's arm in a death grip. "You'd better be right about those mass murderers, Gracie Lynn. I can't run in five-inch heels."

Gracie could've pointed out that the heels hadn't been her idea. Savannah had insisted they dress for their covert mission in solid black. While Gracie wore a regular black t-shirt, jeans, and boots, Savannah wore a silk designer jumpsuit and heels that looked more appropriate for a cocktail party.

"How are we going to get in?" Savannah asked in a hushed voice.

Gracie whispered back. "We're going to use a key." She clicked on the flashlight Emery had given her and pointed it down to a large rock by the front porch steps. Unfortunately, when she lifted the rock, there was only a family of roly-poly bugs under it.

"Oooh!" Savannah jumped back.

Gracie replaced the rock and swept the beam of light over the ground, but she didn't find the key. She was about to abort the mission when she remembered Dirk using a window to get into Becky and Mason's house. "Let's look and see if there's a window open."

Both front windows turned out to be locked tight, but the bedroom window in the back slid open with only a little effort.

"I'll need a boost," Gracie said.

Savannah bumped her out of the way with her hip. "No, ma'am. You aren't climbing in any windows. I'd never forgive myself if you reinjured your back. I'll climb in." She grabbed onto the windowsill and hoisted herself up. She only got halfway in before her lower half got stuck. Her legs flailed around, one high heel flying off and barely missing Gracie's head.

Gracie picked up the shoe. "Are you stuck?"

A familiar and heart-stopping voice spoke from behind her. "I think the answer to that question would be 'yes.'"

Gracie turned to see Dirk standing only a few feet away, wearing nothing but a pair of faded jeans with the top button undone. "Dirk," she breathed.

In the beam of the flashlight, his muscled chest and washboard abdomen looked even more defined than it had at the motor lodge. With the button open, his jeans hung low, revealing pale skin that was untouched by the sun. A line of dark hair ran from his navel to the open vee of his jeans.

He cleared his throat, and she suddenly realized where she was shining the flashlight. She quickly lowered it to the ground as her face filled with heat. "What are you doing here?" she asked. "I thought you left."

"Leaving Bliss seems to be harder than I expected." His voice didn't hold annoyance, just resignation. "I'm going to assume that you're looking for another Tender Heart chapter."

Before she could answer, Savannah spoke. "Sweet Baby Jesus!"

Gracie turned to her friend and noticed that a light was now on in the bedroom. And since it was doubtful that Savannah could reach a light, someone had to be in the room with her. She looked back at Dirk and couldn't keep the hurt and annoyance from her voice. "You brought Winnie here?"

Dirk opened his mouth to answer when Savannah started kicking her legs. "Call the cops! There's a perverted bum living in Raff's cabin."

Dirk laughed as Gracie headed for the front door. He easily caught up with her. "Slow down or you're going to get another muscle cramp. Savannah's not in any danger."

"I haven't had a muscle cramp since the last one. And what is going on? Why are you here? And who's in Raff's cabin?"

He took her arm as they climbed the porch steps. He hadn't touched her since the kiss, and the feel of his warm fingers on the underside of her arm made her a little clumsy. The toe of her cowboy boot caught the top step, and she stumbled. His fingers tightened as he kept her from doing a face plant onto the porch.

"You okay?" He turned her to face him. The light from the open door reflected in his concerned gray eyes, and she couldn't help the words that popped out of her mouth.

"I missed you."

The concern in his eyes was replaced with a look she couldn't define. He started to say something when Savannah yelled.

"Don't you dare touch me!"

Gracie hurried in the open door and straight to the bedroom. Savannah was still stuck in the window, the low neckline of her jumpsuit showing more than a little cleavage to the man who was sitting on the hope chest at the foot of the bed. Regardless of the longer hair and the scruff and the new tattoo, Gracie recognized him immediately.

"Raff?"

He turned. "Gracie Lynn?" His endearing half-smile lifted one side of his mouth as he got to his feet and pulled her into his arms. He drew back and gave her a thorough onceover. "I must say you look a helluva lot better than you did last time I saw you, Baby Girl."

"And you look like a mountain man." She tugged on a strand of his long hair.

He winked. "I did spend a little time in the mountains."

"I hate to interrupt a family reunion," Savannah said, "but if y'all don't mind . . ."

Gracie hurried over to her friend. "Oh my gosh, I'm so sorry, Savannah. Here, take my hands and I'll try to pull you in."

Dirk walked over. "I've seen the situation from both sides, and I don't think that's going to work."

Savannah eyes widened. "Are you saying I'm too fat to fit through the window, Dirk Hadley?"

"No, ma'am. I'm saying that the window is too small for your . . . abundant beauty."

Raff snorted. "In other words, your butt is too big to fit."

Savannah turned on Raff. Gracie had never seen her look so mean. Even when she talked about Miles leaving her at the altar, her eyes hadn't crackled with so much fire. "Didn't your mama ever teach you that it's extremely rude to talk about a lady's bee-hind?"

Raff tipped his head. "Yes, ma'am, she sure did. She also taught me that a true lady would never enter a man's bedroom without an invitation." He walked out of the room. Less than a minute later, Savannah released a startled squeal before she disappeared from the window. When Raff returned, he had her slung over his shoulder. He dumped

her unceremoniously on the bed before he turned
to Gracie. "Okay, Baby Girl, you want to tell me
why you're sneaking around after midnight with
this redheaded vixen?"

"Vixen!" Savannah sat up. With her long hair
spilling around her in fiery waves and her blue eyes
snapping, she did look a little like a vixen. "I'll have
you know I was born and raised a southern lady
and am no more a vixen than—"

Raff held a finger to his lips. Savannah closed her
mouth with a snap and glared at him. The glare
turned to wide-eyed surprise when he lifted the
lid of the hope chest and pulled out a manila envelope.

He held it up. "I'm going to assume that you and
the vixen were searching for this."

*"The gun pointed straight at Johnny's heart stopped him in his tracks. 'You want to explain why you've been following me?' Dax asked. Before Johnny could come up with a reply, Daisy came flying down from the stable's hayloft like an avenging angel and landed on Dax. It was just bad timing that Johnny's brother, Rory, walked in at that moment."*

# CHAPTER FOURTEEN

✿

"**W**HY DIDN'T YOU TELL SAVANNAH and Gracie who I am?" Dirk waited to ask the question until after Gracie's car had disappeared around the bend.

Raff stared out at the road for a moment before he looked at Dirk. He didn't answer the question. Instead, he hauled off and punched him. And Raff had one rock solid punch. Dirk's ears were still ringing long after he caught his balance.

"What the hell was that for?"

"For screwing around with your cousin." Raff strode into the cabin. Dirk tested his jaw before he followed.

"First of all, Gracie isn't my cousin. And second, I didn't screw around with her."

Raff turned and stared him down. "I'm not talking about sex. There's more than one way to screw over a women. When you were filling me in on everything that's been going on in Bliss while I've been gone, you failed to mention that Gracie is in love with you."

"She's not in love with me!" He realized he was yelling and lowered his voice. "It's just a crush. Gracie was lonely for company when I started working at the Arrington Ranch. She got confused about her feelings is all."

"She didn't look confused tonight. She looked like she knew exactly what she wanted." His eyes narrowed. "You."

It was the truth. There had definitely been a switch in the way Gracie looked at him. Before her eyes had been filled with adoration. Then after Winnie, they'd been filled with hate. Now they were filled with desire . . . and something else that he refused to name. When she'd first seen him outside the window, she'd breathed his name as if she'd been holding her breath ever since he'd left. It had hit him like a punch in the heart and knocked him off balance. He was still struggling to find his equilibrium.

"It doesn't matter how she looks at me," he said. "There's nothing between us. And there's not going to be. I'm leaving."

Raff stared at him for a moment before he walked into the kitchen. He returned with two cans of cold beer. He handed one to Dirk. "Hold that on your chin."

Dirk took the can and sat down on the couch. Since arriving at the Tender Heart Ranch that morning, Raff had bombarded him with questions. It turned out that Raff was the man who had shown up at Granny Bon's house with the birth certificate. While she hadn't told him she was adopted, she *had* bragged about her grandchildren and shown him pictures. Raff had recognized Dirk when he drove past him. It didn't help that Dirk had introduced himself.

He held the can to his jaw. "You Arringtons are a violent bunch."

"It's in the blood." Raff flopped down on the couch next to him and popped open his can of beer. "And what do you mean 'you Arringtons?' Are you telling me you don't have a temper?"

He thought about fighting with his father the day before in Cole's barn. "Only when pushed to my limit."

Raff glanced over and spoke solemnly. "Gracie is my limit. She's had one hell of a life and I'm not just talking about the accident. Her mother abandoned her when she was just a baby and never once contacted her. She doesn't even know who her father is. And Uncle Hef . . ." He left the sentence hanging. Dirk should've left it alone. But where Gracie was concerned, he couldn't seem to leave anything alone.

"Did Cole's father love her?"

Raff took a deep drink of beer. "I think he tried. But he loved Gracie's mom so damned much it was hard for him to look at Gracie without thinking about 'the other man.' I think that's why the rest of us worked so hard to make Gracie feel loved." He glanced at Dirk. "I get why your grandmother didn't want you to tell anyone why you were here.

But when you saw Gracie getting attached, you should've confided in her."

Dirk popped open the beer and took a drink. "Don't you think she'll be even more hurt when she discovers that Lucy isn't the saint she thinks she is? It will devastate her to find out her idol dropped off her child without a second glance just like her mother dropped her off."

Raff studied his bare feet that were propped on the coffee table. "Damn. I guess I didn't give that much thought when I went on my quest to find your grandmother. But Gracie is stronger than she looks. She'll be strong enough to deal with the truth."

Dirk took another sip of beer and propped his feet next to Raff's. "Your limit is Gracie. Mine is my Granny Bon. She's the rock that holds my family together. She never asked me for anything until she asked me to find out the truth about her mother. And if she doesn't want that truth to get out, then it's not getting out."

"The truth always has a way of getting out."

Dirk couldn't disagree, but he couldn't give in either. They sat there staring at their feet for a long while before he spoke. "Where did you get the certificate anyway?"

"The same place I found the chapter. In Lucy's hope chest. It was one of the few things that survived the fire that destroyed the house my father built after the Arrington brothers split the ranch." Dirk was curious about the fire, but he was more curious about the birth certificate. So he kept his mouth shut and let Raff continue.

"After the accident, I wanted to give Gracie

something that would make her feel like she was part of the family. She'd always loved the hope chest my dad inherited from Lucy, so I decided to restore it and give it to her. When I was sanding it, I discovered a hidden compartment in the bottom. It was there that I found your grandmother's birth certificate." He glanced over. "Tonight I went to put the certificate back in the compartment and I found the chapter to the last Tender Heart book."

Dirk lowered the can of beer and looked at him. "Which means someone else knows about the secret compartment."

"It would appear that way."

"It would have to be someone close to Lucy." A thought struck him. "Do you think it could be Lucy's lover—my great-grandfather?"

He hadn't told Raff about Lucy's diary. He felt like that would be betraying Becky and Gracie's trust. Although stealing the diary had been a pretty big betrayal, and he wasn't sure why he hadn't left it in the backpack with the chapters he gave to Gracie. Maybe because he wanted his grandmother to have something from her mom. It certainly wasn't because he wanted something. He wanted nothing from his great-grandmother.

"It makes sense," Raff said. "It also makes sense that if Lucy loved him, she would've given him the final book."

"But why is he hiding the chapters now?"

"I don't know. Maybe he didn't want to share the book before because it was the only thing he had from Lucy. Maybe before he dies he wants the book to be published—without making the connection between him and Lucy."

It was funny, but Dirk had spent so much time and energy on hating Lucy that he hadn't given much thought to his great-grandfather. Now he realized that two people were to blame for his Granny Bon becoming an orphan.

He set the can of beer on the coffee table a little harder than was necessary. "That's chicken shit."

Raff lifted an eyebrow at him and smiled. "You don't have a temper, huh?"

"Only when provoked. And I think I have a right to be pissed at a father and mother for leaving an innocent baby at an orphanage. I could understand if they didn't have money to take care of my grandmother. But at the time, the Arringtons had plenty of money."

"I don't think it was about money. Back then, young women were ostracized for having babies out of wedlock. Especially in a small town like Bliss."

Dirk got to his feet. "Then the asshole should've married her."

While Dirk was raring for an argument, Raff casually tossed his beer can at the trashcan. From all the rumors he'd heard, Dirk had thought that Raff was a hotheaded bad boy who reacted before he thought things through. He didn't seem like that to Dirk. He rubbed his sore jaw. At least, not unless provoked.

"Maybe he couldn't. Maybe he was already married," Raff said.

Dirk thought of all the old married men in Bliss and tried to figure out who could've been Lucy's lover. Who would be the right age? Who was the most attached to the Tender Heart series and Lucy?

Who was cold enough to abandon their child?

"If he spent all this time hiding the chapters, why wouldn't he spend some time looking for my grandmother?" he asked.

"Adoption files are sealed. Even with the Internet, I spent months checking out leads on babies that were born in Houston on that day. Of course, it wouldn't have taken me so long if your grandmother had been truthful about being adopted." He got to his feet. "I'm going to bed. If you still want to leave, I'll drive you into Austin in the morning."

Once Raff left the room, Dirk stood there fuming for a few minutes before the photographs on the shelves by the fireplace grabbed his attention. The top shelf held old sepia-toned photographs of unsmiling couples in old-fashioned clothes. They were no doubt Dirk's ancestors, but he didn't have a clue who they were. On the second shelf, he recognized Lucy in some of the photographs. She hadn't been beautiful. But she'd been striking with her black hair and deep blue eyes, which held an aloof sadness. The only picture he'd seen of Lucy smiling was the one he'd found in a box at Ms. Marble's house.

The sensual smile in the picture was the first clue that she might've had a lover. Although if he were honest, he didn't need the picture or the diary or the dedication page to know he was her great-grandson. The moment he'd stepped into Bliss, he'd had a gut feeling.

He lowered his gaze to the picture on the next shelf. He recognized Zane's father sitting astride a huge stallion next to two men on horseback who had to be Cole's and Raff's fathers. They made an imposing trio in their leather chaps and cowboy hats. And staring at the picture, Dirk couldn't help but wonder how different his grandmother's life would've been if Lucy had acknowledged her. How different his mother's life would've been if she'd had Lucy's money to pay for better medical care. Would they have caught the ovarian cancer earlier if they'd known that's what his mother's grandmother had died from?

These questions and a lot more circled his head as he stared at the pictures. Including how his life might've been different. If he'd had strong male role models, would he have turned into such a belligerent teen after his mother died?

His gaze landed on the pictures on the last shelf. These were newer photographs. One of Becky riding a motorcycle and splattered in mud from her helmet to her boots. Another of Raff, Zane, and Cole. They were much younger and dressed in swim trunks. They had their arms linked and were holding up what looked to be Indian arrowheads. The last picture was of Gracie. There had been no pictures of her on horseback in Cole's house. It was understandable. Cole didn't want his sister being reminded of the accident. So Dirk had never seen Gracie on a horse. The photograph blindsided him.

Whoever had taken the picture knew how to take an action shot. They'd caught Gracie and the horse just as they rounded the barrel and were headed for the wire. The horse's legs weren't even touching the ground. Its coat was slick with sweat. Its mane was flying.

And then there was Gracie. While most people

rode a horse, Gracie became one with it. From the way she sat in the saddle to the way she leaned over Brandy's neck. Her turquoise eyes sparkled with excitement and her jaw was set. Her pink felt cowboy hat was tugged low, and her hair waved behind her like silvery wheat in the moonlight.

She had always been pretty, but in this picture she was breathtakingly stunning. And happy. Happier than he'd ever seen her. He'd just accepted her fear of horses as a result of the accident. He'd never realized what that fear had cost her. He realized it now, and it made his heart hurt.

"Turn off the damned light!" Raff's loud bellow cut through his thoughts.

Dirk gave the picture one last glance before he walked to the couch. But long after he turned off the lamp, he could still see Gracie barrel-racing with her eyes sparkling and her hair waving. Everyone thought she was fine now that she could walk again. But she didn't just need to learn how to walk.

She needed to learn how to fly.

*"The gunshot made the entire town come running. By the time Daisy's ears stopped ringing, the sheriff was arresting Dax, the doctor was directing Johnny and his brother Duke to carry Rory to his house, and the rest of the folks were hailing Daisy as a hero. And there was no way a hero could sneak out of town."*

# Chapter Fifteen

&

"SWEET BABY JESUS, IS THE sun brighter in Texas?"

Gracie had to bite back a smile when Savannah staggered into the kitchen looking the worse for wear. She wore two different house slippers, her blue silk kimono wasn't tied correctly, her red hair shot out from her head like a lion's mane, and her eyes were covered by huge designer sunglasses.

"I believe it's called a hangover." Emery got up from the table where she had been examining the Tender Heart chapter that Raff had found. "That's what happens when you drink an entire bottle of wine."

Savannah plopped down on a stool at the breakfast bar. "I did not drink the entire bottle. Gracie helped me."

"That's right, I did." Gracie didn't mention that she'd only taken a few sips as she continued to stir the scrambled eggs she was making for breakfast. Dirk was the one who had taught her how to make scrambled eggs. *Low and slow is the way to go.* But as his words popped into her head, she didn't think about cooking eggs as much as his hands sliding over her body. She blinked away the image. "You want some eggs, Savannah?"

Savannah's face turned a shade paler, and she shook her head. "No, thank you, Sweet Pea. But I would give my two-carat diamond earrings for a cappuccino."

"Sorry," Emery placed a cup in front of her, "all we have is plain coffee, but I did add plenty of vanilla creamer."

"You are an angel from heaven, Em." Savannah took a sip and sighed. After another sip, she glanced over at the pages of the book spread out on the top of the table. "So is it authentic?"

Emery hesitated for only a second before a smile brightened her face. "It certainly—"

The back door flew open, and Carly came striding in with a plastic-wrapped plate. "Sorry I couldn't get here sooner. The diner was a madhouse this morning, and since Dirk has left town, I'm struggling to keep up. The Sanders sisters spend more time arguing than they do cooking. I think I'm going to split them up between breakfast and dinner shifts." She set the plate on the counter and unwrapped it to reveal cinnamon swirl muffins. "Ms. Marble baked these this morning and I figured Savannah's sweet tooth might need filling."

Emery winked at Carly. "I think the only thing

Savannah can handle this morning is coffee."

Carly looked at Savannah. "Ahh, a little hung over, are we? I hope you were celebrating rather than drowning your sorrows. The best thing to ever happen to you was Miles calling off the wedding."

Savannah's bottom lip protruded. "How can you say that, Carly Sue? I loved Miles. He was everything I ever wanted in a man. He was an intelligent, generous, well-mannered—"

"Butthole."

Savannah pushed down her sunglass to glare at her. "I was going to say refined gentlemen. Unlike that horrid cousin of Cole and Zane's. And Dirk didn't leave town. He's staying in that rundown shack of Raff's."

"Dirk didn't leave?" Carly said. "But why would he say he was leaving and then not?" It was a good question. One Gracie had never gotten an answer to. It was hard to think when Dirk didn't have a shirt on.

"I don't have a clue," Savannah said. "Or what he was doing at Raff's—besides lookin' mighty fine." She glanced over at Gracie and winked. "Isn't that right, Gracie Lynn?"

Gracie couldn't help the heat that filled her cheeks. Dirk had looked more than just fine. He'd looked delectable. But she didn't exactly want to talk about it in front of her sister-in-law who would then talk about it with Cole. Her brother had always worried about Gracie's feelings for Dirk, and Cole had enough to worry about.

"I think Raff is cuter," she lied as she plated some eggs for Emery.

Savannah snorted. "If you like overdeveloped

muscles and god-awful tattoos. And even if I did find his body slightly attractive, his ill-mannered rudeness wouldn't be worth it."

Carly laughed. "It sounds like you and Raff really hit it off. Now I'm dying to meet this man." She glanced at Emery. "We should've gone with them, Em, instead of being old married ladies and staying home."

Emery took the plate of eggs Gracie handed her. "It was probably a good thing I didn't go. I've been extremely tired lately. I fell into bed last night before nine and was out like a—" She glanced at the eggs, and her face turned whiter than Savannah's. "Excuse me." She held a hand over her mouth as she jumped up and raced out of the room.

Carly exchanged looks with Savannah. "Are you thinking what I'm thinking?"

"Sweet Baby Jesus," Savannah breathed.

Carly laughed. "I think you mean Sweet Baby Arrington." She followed after Emery.

When she was gone, Gracie turned to Savannah. "Emery's pregnant? But I didn't even know they were trying."

"I don't think they were." Savannah downed the last of her coffee before she slipped off the barstool. "Do you have any saltine crackers and ginger ale? My Auntie Rue said she lived on saltines and ginger ale when she was first pregnant. And she would know. She was pregnant nine times."

By the time Gracie and Savannah got to the master bathroom with the crackers and ginger ale, Emery was sitting on the lid of the toilet with her face pressed into a wet washcloth. Carly was sitting on the edge of the bathtub trying to console her.

"I'm sure Cole will be happy, Em. He's a good man who will make a great father."

Emery spoke into the washcloth. "Of course he will. But just not now. You know how hard he's working to start the horse ranch. And then there are Gracie's doctor's bills. He hasn't even finished paying off the hospital bills. And yesterday we got the bill from the rehabilitation center."

Carly glanced up and saw Gracie and Savannah standing there. She opened her mouth to say something, but there was nothing to say. Emery was right. Cole wouldn't be happy about the baby. Not when he was drowning under all of Gracie's medical bills.

Gracie handed the crackers to Savannah and headed for the front door. By the time she got in her car, tears were rolling down her cheeks. They weren't sad tears as much as frustrated ones. It was frustrating to have such little control over your life.

Savannah came out the front door and called to her, but she ignored her and took off down the road. She drove until she reached a cluster of trees, then she parked and got out. She walked along the worn path to the open field. In the springtime, the field was filled with bluebonnets. But the blu-ish-purple blooms were long gone and the field was now a lush green from the late August rains. In the midst of the green sat the little white chapel. Just the sight of the church usually calmed Gracie. But today she was too upset to even want to go inside. So she skirted around the church and headed to the cemetery behind it.

The cemetery was located under massive oak trees that had been there much longer than the

Arringtons that were buried beneath. Once inside the gate, she headed to Lucy's gravestone. The gravestone had been appropriately cut into the shape of an open book with the inscription on the pages. But today a woman in a sunbonnet obscured the engraved words.

"Ms. Marble?" Gracie said. Ms. Marble had been Gracie's first grade teacher. From the moment Gracie stepped into the classroom, Ms. Marble had become the strong female figure a motherless six-year-old needed in her life. Since then, the older woman always seemed to be there when Gracie needed her.

Like now.

Ms. Marble turned. "Thank goodness. I knelt down to pick weeds and I can't seem to get up." She smiled. "It appears that you gave up your walker around the time that I might have to get one. Or maybe I should just give up kneeling for long periods of time."

Gracie walked over and held out a hand. "Let me help you."

The woman placed her white-gloved hand in Gracie's. "Now don't be throwing out your back."

She doubted that Ms. Marble's weight would cause anyone to throw out their back, but she braced herself against the tombstone and used her arm strength rather than her back muscles. Once Ms. Marble was on her feet, she still seemed a little wobbly, so Gracie led her over to a stone bench to sit down.

She looked up at Gracie, her eyes sharp beneath the big brim of the straw hat. "Would you like to talk about it?"

Gracie wiped the tears that were still on her cheeks and sat down next to her. "I'm a burden to Cole." She didn't know what she expected, but it wasn't agreement.

Ms. Marble nodded. "Well, of course you are." When Gracie looked at her with surprise, she smiled. "All of us become burdens during our lives. It's part of God's lesson to us and to the people who need to carry us during that time. Before David passed away from cancer, he became a burden. But a burden I was happy to carry because, at one point in my life, he needed to carry me. That's what being a family is all about. Taking turns carrying each other when you're too weak to go on—either physically or mentally."

"But I'm always the one who needs carrying," she said. "Cole has always watched out for me. He took care of me when I was sick and was at the hospital every day after the accident."

Ms. Marble nodded. "He certainly is one of the best big brothers I've ever seen. While other boys his age were ignoring their little sisters, he always seemed to have time for you. I remember him riding you into town every Saturday on the handlebars of his bicycle when you were kids and buying you a cone at the diner."

Gracie released a frustrated sigh. "I wish a cone was all he had to buy me now."

"I guess you're talking about your doctor's bills." When Gracie nodded, she waited a long moment before she spoke. "And what's stopping you from helping Cole pay those bills?"

She paused for only a second before she confided in Ms. Marble. "I'm hoping to find the other chapters in the final Tender Heart book."

Ms. Marble rolled her eyes. "Running around looking for chapters of a book isn't a plan. It's a pipe dream. You were one of the brightest students in your first grade class. You weren't just intelligent. You were creative. You can certainly figure out how to help Cole pay a few bills."

"I don't just need to find a job. I need to find a place to live." It was hard to get the words out. The ranch was the only home she'd ever known. The only place she felt secure and loved. But it was time for her to go. Past time. Cole was starting a family, and he didn't need his baby sister clinging to him. Leaving the ranch she'd spent her entire life on wouldn't be easy, but it was something she needed to do. For Cole. And for herself.

"Since jobs and inexpensive places to live aren't exactly growing on trees in Bliss," she said. "I'll probably have to move."

Ms. Marble shook her head. "I can't see Cole letting you leave Bliss. Nor can I see you being happy away from your family." Her eyes narrowed in thought before she smiled. "I think we can come up with a better solution than that. How are you at baking?"

"About as good as I am at cooking. Not good, but not as bad as Becky."

A look of determination entered Ms. Marble eyes. "Well, then I'll have to teach you. Since I started baking at the diner, more and more people want me to bake cakes and cupcakes for their special occasions. But with the baked goods I make for the diner, I just don't have the time. What about if you help me with the baking and I'll pay you and let you live in the apartment above my garage? At one time it was David's painting studio so it has a bathroom and small kitchenette. Now I use it for storage. But I'll warn you. It will take some major elbow grease to get it in living condition. I offered it to Dirk once, but he graciously declined." She laughed. "I think the clutter was too much for him."

It took Gracie a moment to reply. She was scared. This would be like giving up her walker. The ranch had always been her security. And she wasn't sure who she would be without it.

As if reading her thoughts, Ms. Marble took her hand and held it between her white-gloved hands. "You can do this, Gracie Lynn Arrington. You can do anything you set your mind to."

Gracie took a deep breath and slowly released it. "It looks like you've got an apprentice baker and a tenant."

Ms. Marble gave her hand a squeeze before her gaze got caught by something over Gracie's shoulder. Her smile got even bigger. "I knew the boy couldn't leave."

Gracie turned to find Dirk standing on the other side of the fence, but it wasn't the hot cowboy in the western shirt and jeans that caused her breath to hitch as much as the horse that stood next to him.

*"Johnny wanted to blame Dax for shooting his brother, but there was only one person to blame. His gaze narrowed on Daisy as she strolled toward him. 'Don't look like such a sourpuss,' she said. 'Especially when I saved your life.' She smiled brightly. 'And I have the perfect way to repay me.'"*

# CHAPTER SIXTEEN

❦

DIRK DIDN'T KNOW WHAT HE was doing. He shouldn't have come to the Arrington Ranch. Hell, he shouldn't even be in Bliss. He should be back in Dallas taking care of business. But this morning when he'd gotten up, he hadn't felt like leaving. He'd felt pissed. Pissed that the Arringtons weren't doing anything to get Gracie back on a horse. He'd told Raff just that, whereupon Raff had shrugged and said, "She'll need someone tougher than me to get her back in the saddle. One pleading look from those big blue eyes, and I'm toast."

That was all it had taken for Dirk to accept the challenge. But now that he was confronted by the stark terror in Gracie's eyes, he had to wonder if he was up for the task. He pinned on a smile and took off his hat.

"Good mornin', ladies."

"Help me out, Gracie. My legs are still a little wobbly," Ms. Marble said, but once they were standing, it didn't look like Gracie was helping Ms. Marble as much as Ms. Marble was helping her. She pulled Gracie toward Dirk and Brandy. "Well, good morning yourself. Rumor has it that you left Bliss." She stopped a few feet from the fence that surrounded the graveyard and sent him a stern look. "Of course, I didn't believe it. I knew you wouldn't leave without saying goodbye."

Feeling duly chastised, he cleared his throat. "No, ma'am."

Ms. Marble nodded her head, causing her bonnet to bounce. "See that you don't." Her sharp gaze went to Brandy, then back to him. Her look of approval made all the reasons he shouldn't be there disappear.

Brandy finally saw Gracie and started whinnying and tossing her head to be released so she could get to her beloved owner. The look of terror in Gracie's eyes intensified. Dirk drew the horse's head closer and whispered soothing words until Brandy calmed. It was heartbreaking how much the horse loved Gracie and it made Dirk even more determined to get the two back together.

"Well, I better be going," Ms. Marble said. "Sam Dixon gave me a bushel of apples, and if I want some apple pies ready for the diner tomorrow, I need to get to peeling and slicing."

With her panicked gaze still on Brandy, Gracie held tight to Ms. Marble's arm. "I'll come with you and help."

Ms. Marble patted her hand. "No, thank you, dear. Tomorrow is soon enough to start your new job." She looked Gracie in the eyes. "Remember, you can do anything you set your mind to." She gave her a brief hug before heading toward the gate. "I just made a batch of your favorite chocolate chip cookies, Dirk. If you stop by later, I'll give you some."

"Thank you, Ms. Marble. I'll be sure to do that." Dirk continued to watch Gracie. She looked like she was ready to bolt at any second. He couldn't let her. He put his hat back on and held the gate open for Ms. Marble.

"You're a good man, Dirk Hadley," she whispered before she headed along the path that led to the chapel. He waited for her to disappear around the corner of the church before he tied Brandy's reins to the gate and stepped inside. He'd only been to the cemetery once before. He'd come to see Lucy's grave and see if he could find any clues to his grandmother's parentage. Instead, he'd found a chapter of the last Tender Heart book.

The thought gave him an idea of how to distract Gracie. He moved closer, but not so close as to obscure her view of Brandy. "I've been thinking," he said. "If whoever is hiding the chapters hid one here, why wouldn't they hide another one? This is where everyone says Lucy got all her characters. Not to mention this is where Gus Arrington's grave is. If they hid one at his house, why not one at his grave?"

Brandy started whinnying again. Being this close to Gracie, Dirk could see that the terror in her eyes was mixed with a whole lot of need. She wanted to go to the horse, but her fear wouldn't let her.

"Well, I think I'll just go take a look at Gus's tombstone," he said. "You want to come?"

He wasn't sure if it was the book or fear of being left with the horse that made her follow him. Probably both. Once they could no longer see Brandy, she visible relaxed. She was walking much better. Still, he shortened his long strides so as not to tire her muscles. He would do whatever it took to get her back on a horse, but there would be no more massages. And definitely no more kisses. He didn't want her getting too attached to him again . . . or maybe he didn't want to be the one getting attached. She was dressed in jeans and a halter top today, and he didn't know what was more distracting, her bare back or her bare shoulders.

She bumped him with one of those shoulders as she steered him around a large gravestone. "Gus's grave is this way."

As he followed her, he couldn't keep his gaze from wandering to her butt. It wasn't full and curvy. It was more compact and toned. And his hands itched to palm each cheek and squeeze to see just how toned.

"I thought you were leaving."

Her words brought him out of his sexual fantasy, and he moved next to her. "I am, but I figured Raff could use a little help cleaning up that shack of his."

She shot him an annoyed look. "It's not a shack. It's a historical cabin."

"A historical cabin that needs a lot of work. Getting rid of the weeds took a full morning. And that was with Cole and Zane's help." He laughed. "I've never seen weed pulling become a competition before."

She smiled. "They've always been competitive. So who won?"

He grinned sheepishly. "I did. You might say I'm a little competitive too." They reached the end of the path, and he glanced around. "Where is Gus's grave?"

"Right there." Gracie pointed to the simple wooden cross. Dirk was surprised. He thought the patriarch of the Arrington family would have a huge headstone with some amazing words of wisdom. Instead just a G and A were carved in the cross.

He walked over to stand in front of it. "This isn't what I expected."

Gracie moved next to him. "It *is* surprising given that he was a titled English nobleman."

"And how do you know that?"

"I did a research paper on him in high school." Dirk could picture her sitting in front of a computer screen searching for any tidbit about Gus. The Arrington legacy meant so much to her. It was like she clung to it as a lifeline. "He didn't own a castle or anything," she continued. "But he was an earl and owned a small estate. I've always wondered why he left when his life in England had to be easier than his life here in Texas."

Dirk thought of his own life. How success had been sweet but a little deflating. He now had enough money that he was more than comfortable, but there was no adventure anymore. No excitement. Maybe that's why he'd stayed so long in Bliss. For a small town, it certainly had a lot going on.

"Maybe he didn't want to live in the idyllic English countryside," he said. "Maybe he liked things a little unpredictable and wild."

She glanced over at him. The sun had risen higher in the sky and now shone through the leaves of the oak tree in spangled dots of light that danced over Gracie's blond hair and perfect features—the smooth skin, high cheekbones, full lips, and turquoise blue eyes. Eyes that seemed to sear right through him.

"Like you?" she said. "Is that why you're leaving? Things were getting too predictable?"

He turned away. "I do hate predictability." He walked around the cross. "It appears that my theory was wrong. There's nowhere to hide a chapter-sized envelope. Unless they buried it with Gus."

"Who do you think it is?" she asked. "Who do you think is hiding the chapters? And why?"

He wanted to tell her about his theory of it being Lucy's lover, but then she would know that he'd read the diary. So he shook his head. "I don't know." He changed the subject. "What's this about you working for Ms. Marble?"

"She's hiring me to help her bake."

"I didn't know you liked to bake."

"I don't. But I need to start paying Cole back all the money he's spent on me. Not that what I make with Ms. Marble will put a dent in my hospital and rehabilitation bills."

He knew that Cole was struggling to get his horse ranch up and running, but he didn't know it had to do with Gracie's hospital bills. "Didn't your insurance cover most of that?"

Her cheeks colored. "After my mother took

most of our savings, my dad let the health insurance lapse for a couple months. Unfortunately, my accident happened in that window of time."

That explained a lot. No wonder Cole was working his ass off and still didn't have enough money to start building his horse stables. He had to pay Gracie's bills first. And Gracie working for Ms. Marble *would* only be a drop in the bucket of major medical expenses.

Dirk couldn't help being pissed all over again at Lucy Arrington. If she'd left even a portion of her royalties to her family, Cole and Gracie wouldn't be in this fix.

"Then I guess we better find the rest of those chapters," he said. "You look on this side of the cemetery and I'll take the other. We'll meet back at the gate. Call out if you find something."

As soon as Gracie disappeared down the path, he pulled out his cellphone and fired off an email. Once it was sent, he did a brief search of the cemetery before he headed back to the gate. He sat down on the stone bench by Lucy's grave and glared at the inscription. *Lucy Arrington, a Tender Heart.* He snorted. Lucy didn't have a tender heart. Her heart was as cold as the granite the words were carved into.

"Why are you riding Brandy?" Gracie spoke behind him.

He turned to see her staring at the horse. Brandy was no longer making a fuss to get to Gracie. The horse just stood there with sad eyes.

As casually as possible, Dirk leaned down and picked a piece of tall grass and chewed on the sweet end. "After our weed picking contest, I came back to the ranch with Cole to see how Savannah was doing. She was worried about you. She told me what direction you headed in, and I figured you'd come to the chapel. When I saw Brandy in the paddock, I thought I'd give her some exercise and save me from walking." He glanced over at her. "But I guess I should've asked you first seeing as how Brandy is your horse."

She looked away from the horse and sat down next to him on the bench. "No, it's fine. She needs someone to exercise her more. Cole is busy with his new purebreds and I . . ." She let the sentence hang. Dirk finished it for her.

"And you want nothing to do with her after the accident."

Her gaze locked with his. "Yes. I want nothing to do with her." When he only looked at her, she grew angry. "What? Aren't you going to tell me that I need to get over my fear and get back in the saddle? That Brandy wasn't responsible for the accident? She was just doing what horses do when they're scared? In fact, she could've been trying to save my life by getting me out of harm's way."

Having grown up with three older sisters, he knew when to keep his mouth shut and let women vent. And Gracie needed to vent before she could start healing.

She got up from the bench and started to pace. "And maybe she was trying to save me, but she didn't. She didn't save me from the pain, or the months of physical therapy, or the damned bills. And I don't ever want to get back in the saddle again." She stopped. "Do you understand? Never."

He took the piece of grass out of his mouth and

nodded. "Fair enough. And for the record, I didn't come here today to get you back in the saddle." It was a half-truth. Eventually, he was going to get her back in the saddle. But today he just wanted her to get used to being around Brandy. "I get why you don't want to ride again." He paused, and then shrugged. "That being the case, why don't you sell her?"

Her reaction was exactly what he'd hoped it would be. She looked as if someone had just asked her to sell her most prized possession. "Sell Brandy?"

He got to his feet and spoke as casually as he could. "It makes sense. You're not ever going to ride her again, and Cole has no plans to use her as a broodmare. So why not sell her and make some money? You could use it to help pay off those doctor's bills."

He watched the turmoil that went on in her pretty eyes. The pain. The confusion. The heart-wrenching desperation. Without saying a word, she whirled and headed for the fence far away from Brandy. She climbed it with no problem at all. Dirk had to hurry to untie Brandy and catch up with her. He stopped her right in front of the chapel.

"Wait, Gracie!" He took her arm and spun her around to face him. And Brandy.

He had been prepared for her fear at being this close to the horse. He was not prepared for her out-and-out panic. Her face lost all color and her quaking trembles vibrated through his hand and all the way down to his toes. She took one startled breath and then stopped breathing completely.

He dropped the reins and took her other arm, blocking Brandy from her view and giving her a little shake. "Breathe, Gracie. Breathe, baby." When she didn't, he did the only thing he could think to do to get her mind off her fear. He kissed her.

As soon as his lips touched hers, she exhaled sharply through her nose. Once she was breathing, he should've pulled back. But it had been too long since he'd lost himself in the wet warmth of her mouth. His hands encircled her waist and pulled her closer as he deepened the kiss and took a full taste of Gracie.

It was like coming home. Like stepping into a cozy place that was his and his alone. He slid his tongue into her mouth, and hers tangled with his in a rush of welcoming heat. Her arms came around his neck and her fingers burrowed into his hair, knocking off his hat. He slid his hands to her butt, squeezing and lifting until her hot center was pressed snuggly against his. The need that filled him took his breath away. And there was little doubt that he would've tried to fill that need if Brandy hadn't interrupted.

The horse slipped its wet nose between them. It took Dirk a moment to catch his balance after the kiss. By that time, Gracie had lost it again. She stood as frozen as a statue with tears dripping down her cheeks while the horse nuzzled her.

Dirk's first instinct was to push the horse back and kiss away every single tear, promising her that she never had to see Brandy again. But he knew that wasn't what she needed. She needed to get through the panic so she could get back to the love. So he waited for a few seconds before he calmly picked up his hat, took the horse's reins, and swung into the saddle. He kept his voice causal as he patted Brandy's neck. "This horse loves you, Gracie. But if you can't love her, you need to let her go."

He clicked Brandy into a walk and headed to the ranch. Before they reached the trees, he glanced back. Gracie had turned to watch them, and even from that distance, he could see the tears shimmering in her eyes. His own words came back to him.

*If you can't love her, you need to let her go.*

*"It was probably a bad idea to pull Johnny in on her scheme to leave Bliss. But if she was going to find adventure in the Wild West, she needed help."*

# Chapter Seventeen

❦

"HE KISSED YOU AGAIN?" SAVANNAH placed a stack of old magazines in a box before sending Gracie a sly smile. "Oh, yes, the man definitely likes you."

"I was panicking over Brandy. He only did it to distract me." She finished taping up the box of Mr. Marble's painting supplies she'd been packing and labeled it with a Sharpie marker before carrying it to the stack of boxes by the door.

Ms. Marble hadn't lied when she said the room over the garage needed cleaning out. It had been filled to the rafters with boxes and clutter and would've taken Gracie days to go through if not for Savannah's help. Savannah might be prissy, but she was one hard worker. Together, they almost had everything organized and labeled so Ms. Marble could figure out what she wanted to keep and what she wanted to get rid of.

"I think he could've come up with another way

to distract you," Savannah said as she picked up a sleeping Miss Pitty out of an empty box and lovingly placed the cat on an old divan in one corner. "Dirk likes kissing you, which is why he keeps doing it."

"Even if he does, it doesn't matter now. He's only staying long enough to help Raff get his place in shape."

Savannah snorted. "In that case, he could be here for years. A wrecking ball wouldn't help that place." She picked up an antique lamp and looked at the bottom. "Ooo, I would love to have this in my home décor shop. I wonder if Ms. Marble would sell this to me along with the dining room set in her garage that she said I could buy. The woman is a bigger hoarder than my Aunt Bessy." She set the lamp down and stepped back to study it on the old dresser. "Or maybe you should keep the lamp right here. Once we get the clutter out and hang a few pictures, this little apartment is going to be adorable." She glanced at Gracie and gave her a thorough onceover. "And after we fix up this place, we need to work on you."

Gracie stopped packing. "Me?"

Savannah lifted an eyebrow. "Don't you think it's time to quit dressing like a ponytailed farm girl and start dressing like the stunningly beautiful woman you are?" She walked over and pulled out Gracie's ponytail holder. "You have amazing hair. And great skin. You just need to learn how to highlight them to their best effect. And I'm just the girl to help you do that. When I'm finished with you, Dirk is going to want a lot more kisses."

"And what if I don't want any more kisses from

Dirk?"

Savannah walked around to face her. "Why in the world wouldn't you want more kisses from a sizzling hot cowboy?"

"Because getting involved with Dirk is a dead end street. He's leaving."

Savannah sighed before she pulled Gracie over to the bed. Once they were seated, she took her hands. "I get that you're an avid Tender Heart fan and want one of Lucy's happily-ever-afters. And one day, I have little doubt that you'll find the right man to give you one. But until you do, there's nothing that says you can't enjoy spending time with a good-looking man like Dirk Hadley. You're young and single. Have some fun. Live a little."

Was Savannah right? Had Gracie spent too much time daydreaming about fictional happy endings rather than living life to the fullest? Were the Tender Heart books just another crutch she was using so she wouldn't have to face the real world?

"How much money would it cost to make me over?" she asked.

Savannah smiled. "Not a dime. Lucky for you, I have plenty of makeup and hair styling products. I also brought along some of my perfect-weight clothes that might fit you." Her brow crinkled. "I was convinced that after Miles ran out on our wedding, I'd lose weight. But I haven't lost a single pound. Probably because I'm a stress eater."

"You don't need to lose weight," Gracie said. "You turn men's heads every time you go to town, while they look at me like their kid sister."

Savannah got up. "Not after I get through with you. Now let's finish up here so we can get started.

I'm leaving tomorrow so that doesn't give us much time."

"You're leaving tomorrow?" Gracie knew that Savannah would have to go back to Atlanta eventually. She just hadn't thought it would be so soon. She had become extremely close to her new friend in the last week and hated to see her go.

Savannah nodded sadly. "I wish I could stay longer, but I need to get back to my business. And since I'll be driving a U-Haul truck with Ms. Marble's dining room furniture, I'll need an extra day."

"But I thought you would stay long enough to help me find the rest of the chapters. And Emery was hoping you'd help her decorate the baby's room."

Savannah pulled open one of the dresser drawers and started boxing the framed pictures inside. "You don't need any help finding the chapters. You know a lot more about Lucy than I do. And it's a little too soon to worry about the baby's room when Emery hasn't even told Cole yet."

"She's going to tell him on Saturday night. She's taking him for a nice dinner in Austin first. I think she's still worried about how he'll react."

"If I know your brother at all, he won't let money issues keep him from being happy about having a sweet baby. He loves his family." Savannah picked up the framed picture in the dresser drawer and studied it. "And speaking of family, who is this handsome cowboy with Ms. Marble? He looks familiar." She started to turn the picture to Gracie when Carly came hurrying in the door.

"Emery just called. She found another chapter!"

Tender Heart trumped everything. Upon hearing the news, Gracie and Savannah left their packing and followed Carly back to the Arrington Ranch. It turned out that the eleventh chapter wasn't that hard to find. Emery had discovered it in the bottom drawer of the desk in her and Cole's room. The same desk Lucy had written the Tender Heart books at.

"I know the envelope wasn't in the drawer before I went to Atlanta," Emery said as she reclined on Gracie's bed next to Miss Pitty.

"Which means it was put there while we were gone." Carly was sitting on the floor sipping the wine Savannah had poured her before they headed to Gracie's room for her makeover. Savannah had already applied a ton of makeup to Gracie and was now curling her hair with a curling iron.

"Who stopped by to see you while everyone was in Atlanta, Gracie?" Savannah asked.

"Cole had just about everyone in town stopping by to check on me."

"Did any of them get out of your sight while they were here?" Emery asked.

Gracie thought for a moment. "I left Mrs. Crawley and Joanna Daily while I went to the kitchen to get them some lemonade. And Ms. Marble and Mr. Sims both used the bathroom while they were here."

"Well, we can rule out Ms. Marble. She thinks the hunt for the book is ridiculous," Carly said. "And I doubt if Mrs. Crawley and Joanna Daily would've had time. That leaves Mr. Sims. And since he's my first choice for Honey Bee, it seems likely."

Gracie glanced over at Emery. "You told her about the diary?" Before Emery could answer, Carly cut in.

"No, Savannah told me."

Gracie looked at Savannah. "You told me your mouth was sealed as tight as a Ziploc bag."

Savannah smiled weakly. "My bags have always had a few air holes."

"Or large gaping rips," Carly said. "But you need to seal those up. Finding out who Lucy's lover is could be the key to finding the remaining chapters. And it's looking more and more likely that it's Mr. Sims. I heard him talking at the diner the other day about living in the Reed house with his second wife."

"Oh, I hope Lucy didn't have sex with him right under his wife's nose," Savannah said.

"Maybe he lived there before he married. Maybe he married someone else and that's what broke Lucy's heart," Emery said. "You need to see if you can get more information out of him, Carly. You're the most likely choice since he comes into the diner every day."

"Will do, but it won't be easy. You have to scream like a banshee to get Mr. Sims to hear you."

"There," Savannah stepped back from Gracie. "You look like a beauty queen. All you need is some high heels and my red dress."

The high heels were too big and the dress too small. The hem barely covered Gracie's backside and the neckline barely covered her boobs. But when Savannah turned her to the mirror, all her misgivings faded.

The woman in red who looked back at her didn't look like her. This woman looked confident . . . and sexy. The short hem made her legs look longer and the neckline made her boobs look bigger. Savannah had fixed her hair so it hung around her shoulders in thick waves and the makeup highlighted her cheekbones, the blue of her eyes, and the fullness of her lips. It had been a long time since Gracie had felt good about herself, and it was hard to keep the tears from welling in her eyes.

"I'm beautiful," she whispered.

Emery and Carly joined her at the mirror.

Emery squeezed her arm. "Or course you are. You've always been beautiful, sweetness. Makeup and a dress aren't what make you beautiful, Gracie Lynn. It's what's inside that counts. Isn't that right, Savannah?"

Savannah shrugged. "Beauty is only skin deep, but it doesn't hurt if your skin looks good too."

Gracie couldn't help it. She burst out laughing. She wasn't just laughing over Savannah's comment. She was laughing because she was happy. Happier than she'd felt in a long time. She'd never thought she'd walk again, but there she was standing in front of a mirror in a sexy dress and high heels. And she'd never thought she'd have more than Becky as a close friend, but now she had these women. These strong, determined, confident women who made her feel strong, determined, and confident too.

She continued to laugh, and her friends joined in. They were laughing so hard that they didn't notice the man standing in the doorway of the room until he spoke.

"It looks like y'all are having quite a party."

Gracie sobered instantly at the sound of Dirk's voice. She turned to find him leaning against the doorjamb with his straw cowboy hat cocked up on his head and his bright smile in place. Like always the smile made her tummy feel all light and airy. Especially when he turned it on her. But as soon as he saw her, the smile fizzled to be replaced with an open-mouthed gape of surprise.

Savannah leaned in and whispered. "What did I tell you?" She turned to the other two women. "Come on, ladies. I think there's another bottle of wine in the fridge with our name on it. And a can of soda with Em's."

The women skirted around Dirk who was still staring at Gracie. Once they were gone, he spoke. "What did you do to yourself?"

She blinked. "Excuse me?"

He moved out of the doorway and waved his hand. "Why are you wearing that dress?" He motioned at her face. "And all that makeup?" He pointed to the high heels. "And why in the hell would you wear heels like that when you just learned how to walk again? For Christ's sake, you could reinjure your spine all over in those stupid spiked deathtraps." He nodded at the bed. "Here, sit down and I'll help you take them off."

She didn't know what ticked her off most. His condescending manner or the fact that he hadn't been the least bit blown away by her in the red dress.

She placed her hands on her hips. "I'm not sitting down because I'm not taking them off. It's my back, and if I want to reinjure it, that's my business. In fact, I was just headed over to the Watering

Hole to try my shoes out on the dance floor." She didn't know where the lie came from, but now that it was out, she was considering doing just that. It had been a long time since she danced.

"Don't be silly, Gracie. You're not ready to dance."

"Really? And how do you know what I'm ready for? Last time I checked, you weren't my physical therapist or my doctor."

He stared at her for a moment before he blew out his breath. "You're right. But if you're going dancing, would you please do it in a normal pair of roper boots? Please."

It wasn't the please as much as the concern in his eyes that had her walking over to the bed. She flopped down and glared at him as she reached down to unbuckle the tiny straps of the high heels.

"Does this make you happy?"

"I won't be happy until those things are off your feet." He took off his hat and knelt on one knee in front of her, removing first one high heel and then the other. It was a scene right out of a fairytale, but Gracie was tired of living in a fairytale. Savannah was right. It was time to release her dreams of a Tender Heart hero and just enjoy a man's company. And the only man she'd ever wanted to enjoy was kneeling right in front of her.

She reached out and smoothed the lock of golden-brown hair off his forehead. He froze, and his gaze slowly slid over her legs and up her body. It stopped on her breasts that rose and fell with her rapid breathing. His hand tightened on her foot, and her nipples tightened against the soft material of the dress. His breath puffed out, part air and part groan, before he released her foot and quickly got his feet.

"I should probably go." He refused to look at her as he rolled the brim of his hat in his hands. "I just wanted to stop by to tell you that I found a buyer for Brandy."

She hadn't felt wobbly while standing in the high heels, but she felt wobbly now. It was like the earth had suddenly tilted and she was sliding off. She knew she needed to sell Brandy. Keeping her was wrong. Especially when she didn't want to even look at the horse. Brandy needed to go to someone who would ride her and groom her . . . and love her as much as Gracie did.

She squeezed her eyes closed to regain her balance and spoke barely above a whisper. "Who wants to buy her?"

There was a long stretch of silence before Dirk answered. "I do."

*"The woman was crazy! Daisy wouldn't last one second in the real 'Wild West.' And someone needed to set her straight. Since she'd tried to save his life, the least Johnny could do was try to save hers."*

# CHAPTER EIGHTEEN

❨

"I TOLD YOU THAT SHE'D AGREE to sell Brandy." Cole leaned over the pool table and took his shot. The ball he was aiming at clipped the edge of the pocket and bounced out to the middle of the table. "Especially when she can't even look at a horse without panicking. Who came up with that lamebrain idea, anyway?"

Raff stepped closer to the table. "That would be me, Cuz. And I still think it's a good idea." He took aim and sent a striped ball careening into the opposite side pocket before he glanced at Dirk. "It must've been the execution that sucked."

Dirk couldn't deny it. His execution *had* sucked. And it was that damned red dress's fault. If she hadn't looked so . . . unlike Sweet Gracie, he would've finessed the situation much better. But the sexy little number had short-circuited his brain. Or maybe what had short-circuited his brain was her body in the dress. Every one of her sweet curves was outlined by the clingy red material. Including her nipples, when they had hardened beneath his gaze.

She desired him. She desired him as much as he desired her. He'd wanted to strip the dress off her body and take her right there on the bed. He glanced at the men he was playing pool with. If the Arrington cousins could read his thoughts, they'd beat him to a pulp. And he deserved it. He had no business thinking about Gracie in those terms. No business at all.

And yet, for the last three nights, all he'd done was lie on Raff's lumpy old couch and think about Gracie. Not just the way she'd looked the other night in the red dress, but also about the way she looked in every other article of clothing he'd seen her in. The pretty pink maid-of-honor's dress at Becky's wedding. The thin blue nightshirt. The tight black t-shirt and jeans she'd worn the night she and Savannah broke into Raff's cabin. The halter top she'd worn in the cemetery.

"Hell, Dirk," Zane interrupted the Gracie Fashion Show. "If you're gonna take this long to take a shot, I'm going to head over to the diner and see if Carly has any leftovers. Tonight's special was meatloaf, and Carly makes the best damned meatloaf on both sides of the Pecos."

"You can say that again," Cole said. "She dropped some by the house for our dinner because Emery hasn't been feeling well."

"Is she okay?" Dirk asked.

Cole hesitated for only a second before dropping a bomb. "I think she's pregnant."

"Holy shit!" Zane leaned his pool cue against the table and walked over to slap Cole on the back. "Congratulations, man. That's great news."

Surprisingly, Cole turned on Zane like a feral dog. "Don't pull that surprised crap with me. Carly already told you that Emery's pregnant, didn't she?"

Zane stared at him with confusion. "What are you talking about? This is the first I've heard of it."

"Bullshit!" Cole tossed his pool cue on the table. "You knew. That's why you paid Gracie's rehabilitation bills. You took pity on me because I'm starting a family. Well, I don't need your fuckin' pity." He shoved Zane back into the barstools. One fell over and Zane tripped over it, landing hard on his ass. The look on his face said that things were about to get ugly.

Dirk dropped his pool cue and came around the table to intervene, but Raff beat him to it and stepped between Cole and Zane.

"That's enough, Zane."

"Me? I didn't start it. Cole did with his groundless accusations."

"They aren't groundless." Cole said. "Who else would pay thousands of dollars worth of Gracie's rehabilitation bills and ask to remain anonymous?"

Raff glanced at Zane. "You didn't pay the bills?"

Zane shook his head. "No, but if I'd known about them, I would've. Especially now that Emery is pregnant." He glared at Cole. "When are you going to stop being such a pigheaded asshole and accept help?"

"I don't need help," Cole snapped. "I can take care of my own family."

"We are your family!"

Raff nodded. "He has a point. The reason our fathers split up the ranch in the first place was because they all thought they could handle things by themselves. But it took a team effort to make the Arrington Ranch the biggest ranch in Texas, and if our fathers could've let go of their egos, it still would be."

Cole released his breath. "I just want to prove I can do it."

"You will," Raff said with such conviction in his voice that it was hard not to believe him. He held up his fist. At first, Dirk thought he wanted the cousins to bump it, but then Zane fished a gold chain out of the collar of his shirt and held up a Native American arrowhead. An arrowhead similar to the one that hung from the leather lacing wrapped around Raff's wrist.

The appearance of the arrowheads took all the fight out of Cole. He reached into his front jean pocket and pulled out his key ring with an arrowhead attached to the ring. "I'm sorry. I guess I get a little crazy about charity."

"I swear I didn't pay the bill, Cole," Zane said.

"Then who did?"

Dirk picked up his beer from a nearby table and finally spoke. "Does it matter? My grandma always said to never look a gift horse in the mouth." He held up the bottle of beer. "To gift horses. And to Cole becoming a daddy."

Cole stared at him for a second before he broke out in a big smile. "I'm going to be a daddy." He punched the air before he glanced at Zane and lifted his eyebrows. "I dare you to top that."

After they finished off their beers and the game

of pool, Cole and Zane made their excuses and headed back to their wives. With no one to go home to, Raff and Dirk stayed at the bar and played another game of pool. Raff was a cutthroat pool player who didn't believe in doing much socializing while he kicked your butt. He waited until he'd almost cleared the entire table of striped balls before he spoke.

"You paid the bill, didn't you?"

Dirk lowered the bottle of beer the waitress had just brought. "Excuse me?"

Raff stared him down as he chalked the tip of his cue. "Gracie's rehab expenses. You paid them."

Dirk snorted. "A drifter like me? Where would I get that kind of money?"

Raff blew the excess chalk off the tip of his pool cue. "Your grandmother didn't like sharing information about herself, but she had no problem bragging about her four grandkids. Especially her grandson who started a little company with his college friend that hooks people up with jobs." He leaned over and hit the last striped ball into a pocket. "I wasn't real curious about what that company was until I met you." He glanced down. "Drifters usually can't afford Lucchese boots." He pointed to a pocket. "Eight ball in the corner pocket." He took aim. "Imagine my surprise when I found out that the little company you started was featured in *Forbes Magazine* as a company to watch."

He hit the eight ball into the corner pocket, then casually walked around the table and placed his stick in the pool cue rack on the wall. When he turned, Dirk expected questions. But Raff never did the expected.

"I talked with your grandmother."

Always protective of Granny Bon, Dirk bristled. "I hope you didn't try to bully her into accepting you as family?"

"I don't think the Hulk could bully your grand-mother. She seems to be more stubborn than Cole is. And I didn't call her about accepting us as family. I called to tell her that I was sending her the birth certificate."

Dirk's shoulders relaxed. "Thank you. I know that will mean a lot to her."

Raff nodded before he grabbed his cowboy hat off a nearby hook. "I still think I had a good idea. Gracie will cave as soon as you arrive to pick up the horse. And once she realizes how much she still loves Brandy, you can start working on getting her back in the saddle."

Dirk walked over and placed his pool cue in the rack next to Raff's. "Once she realizes how much she loves the horse, I'm out of here. You and your cousins can take it from there. I'm done with this town." He turned to find Raff leaning on the pool table with a big grin on his face. Or his version of a grin. With his scar, it was more of a sneer.

"That's bullshit, and you and I both know it. Go ahead and act like you can't wait to get out of here, but Bliss has hooked you. And I can sympathize. I've tried time and time again to shake the dust of this two-bit town off my boots, but I always end up coming back."

"Because you have family here."

Raff studied him. "So do you."

Dirk didn't know how to respond to that so he

didn't even try. "If I'm going to convince Gracie that I really want to buy Brandy, I'll need to borrow your truck and that old horse trailer you keep behind the barn. It needs new tires, but I can have Cole put those on tomorrow, then I'll head over to the Arrington Ranch right after."

"I'd call before you go to make sure she's there. She's been helping Ms. Marble bake during the day and fixing up that room over the garage in the evenings." His brows knitted. "I'm like Cole. I'm not real thrilled about her moving out. But with the baby coming, I get why she's doing it. Still, it has to be hard moving away from the only home she's ever known."

Raff's words stayed with Dirk as they paid their bills and headed for Raff's truck in the parking lot. They had almost reached it when Dirk stopped short.

"You go on," he said. "I'll catch a ride out later. There's something I need to do."

Dirk waited for Raff to pull out of the Watering Hole's parking lot before he headed toward Ms. Marble's house. The house with its peaked roof and intricately carved corbels looked like something Ms. Marble had baked in her oven. The brown siding resembled gingerbread and the white trim icing. A white picket fence surrounded blooming flowerbeds and a deep front porch. Since there wasn't a porch light on, he didn't realize Ms. Marble was sitting there until she spoke.

"I'm going to assume that you didn't come to see me."

He took off his hat. "Good evening, Ms. Marble."

"More like night, Mr. Hadley." Her rocking chair

creaked. "It seems that men these days haven't been taught the appropriate times to come courting."

He smiled as he moved his hat over his heart. "Are you rejecting my suit because of the time, Ms. Marble?" It was too dark on the porch to see her, but he could hear the laughter in her voice.

"You are a charming one, I'll give you that. As charming as my first husband, but we both know you haven't come to court me as much as Gracie."

Her words took the smile from his face, and he tugged his hat back on. "I'm not courting Gracie. I just stopped by to see if she needed any help cleaning out her new apartment. Last time I saw it, it had more boxes than a warehouse."

"Which was why you declined my offer to live there."

He'd declined the offer because he hadn't wanted Ms. Marble keeping track of his every move. The woman was too smart for her own good. "I've never liked clutter," he said. "I thought Gracie could use some help moving some of those boxes."

The rocker creaked back and forth for a long moment. "Well, I'm sure that strapping young man who's up there now can lift a few boxes."

Dirk should've known that Cole or Zane would stop by to help her. "Since she's got her cousins, I guess I'll just be on my way. Goodnight, Ms. Marble." He tipped his hat before pulling it on and heading back the way he'd come. Ms. Marble's words stopped him.

"Unless the Arringtons no longer drive trucks, it's not her cousins."

Dirk turned to the garage and finally noticed the blue Equinox parked behind Gracie's Malibu. The other night when she'd said she was going dancing at the Watering Hole, he hadn't been too worried. Except for Twofer Tuesday when drinks and wings were two for one, the bar was never busy. Usually, the only men to dance with were old guys who would rather drink and discuss sports with Hank the bartender than two-step.

But as he stared at the blue car, he realized his mistake. And he couldn't help the flood of jealousy that rushed through him at just the thought of a man dancing with Gracie in her sexy red dress. Without saying another word to Ms. Marble, he headed for the garage. He took the stairs two at a time, and when he reached the door, he didn't stop to knock. He turned the knob and waltzed right in.

The sight that greeted him sent his blood to a rolling boil. The strapping young man had Gracie pinned to the floor, and she didn't look happy about it. Her face was scrunched in pain. Dirk didn't hesitate to grab the man by the collar and waistband and toss him against the wall before slamming a forearm against his throat.

"Say your prayers, you sonofabitch, because those are the last words you're going to get out before I kick your ass."

"Dirk!" Gracie grabbed his arm and tried to pull him off. "What are you doing? Have you lost your mind?"

"He was touching you," he growled.

She continued to tug at his arm. "Of course, he was touching me. He's my physical therapist!"

The words cut through his red haze, and he finally noticed the name stitched over the front pocket of the navy polo shirt the guy was wearing. *Lone Star Health*. Dirk removed his arm from the man's throat and let him slide down the wall as he turned to Gracie. "He's your physical therapist?"

Gracie ignored the question and knelt next to the guy. "Oh my God, Calvin. Are you okay? Can you breathe? Do I need to call an ambulance?"

Calvin took a few uneven breaths and rubbed his throat. "No, I'm okay." He glanced up at Dirk. "What is your problem, man?"

It was a good question. One he couldn't answer. He held out a hand to help him up, but Calvin ignored it and got to his feet. He walked over and grabbed the duffel bag that sat on the floor by the door. When it was hooked over his shoulder, he turned to Gracie. "I think it's best if you change to a woman therapist. Male therapists don't work with jealous boyfriends." He walked out the door.

As soon as he was gone, Gracie turned to him. She was wearing black yoga pants and a pink skinny-strapped athletic top that showed off her shoulders and the curve of her breasts. The outfit wasn't nearly as sexy as the red dress, but desire still punched him hard in the stomach.

Her confused look said she wanted answers, but damned if he could give her any. He didn't understand why this woman pulled so many emotions out of him. Or maybe he just didn't want to understand. He needed to leave. He couldn't stay any longer. Not only because his life was elsewhere, but also because if he stayed, the truth would eventually come out. Finding out about Lucy would kill Gracie, but damned if leaving wasn't killing him.

He grabbed his hat off the floor. "I'll be by to

pick up Brandy tomorrow before I leave town."
He walked out the door.

*"Wild West Lesson 1: Shooting a gun is harder than it looks . . . especially with a handsome cowboy standing behind you whispering instructions in your ear."*

# Chapter Nineteen

❦

GRACIE SPENT SATURDAY MORNING IN Ms. Marble's kitchen helping her bake four dozen cupcakes for Mrs. Crawley's three-year-old granddaughter's birthday party. Gracie usually enjoyed chatting with Ms. Marble while they baked, but today she was too distracted to keep up a conversation. Fortunately, Ms. Marble figured that out and left Gracie to her thoughts.

Those thoughts centered around two things: Brandy and Dirk. Or more specifically Brandy and Dirk leaving. She thought she'd felt depressed when Dirk left the first time. It would be nothing compared to how depressed she would be when he left this time. Because this time he would be taking her horse.

She knew it was for the best. Just the sight of Brandy brought back all the pain. Not just the physical pain, but also the mental pain of being in a wheelchair and losing the only father she'd ever known. And yet, she still loved Brandy. It had killed her to see the desperate plea in the horse's deep brown eyes at the chapel.

Brandy would be so much better off with Dirk. There was little doubt that he would love her and care for her. But deep in Gracie's heart, she knew Brandy would never be completely happy with anyone else. Horses formed bonds just like people did. Over the years, she and Brandy had become a team. And nothing could replace what they'd had. Not even a kind, caring man like Dirk.

Although Dirk hadn't been so kind and caring last night. He'd been jealous. It seemed that Savannah was right. Dirk was interested in her as more than just a friend. But it didn't look like that would stop him from leaving.

When she and Ms. Marble finished the cupcakes, they boxed them so Gracie could deliver them to the Crawley house for the party. It was just her luck that Winnie answered the door.

"Well, if it isn't Little Miss Goody Two Shoes."

Gracie was too depressed to even attempt a smile. "Hi, Winnie. I brought the cupcakes for Lily Anna's birthday party."

"I heard you were working for Ms. Marble. I bet you just love making sugary sweet treats to go with your sugary sweet personality." Winnie smiled slyly. "It's too bad that Dirk Hadley doesn't care for all that sugar. Too bad he likes his women a little spicier."

Gracie had the sudden desire to open up the box of cupcakes and smash them right into Winnie's gloating face. She might've done it if Winnie's older sister, Debbie Lee, hadn't shown up.

"Stop being such a bitch, Winnie." Debbie Lee shoved her sister out of the doorway. "Now go help Mama with the decorations. The party starts in less than an hour, and we're not nearly ready."

Winnie shot Gracie a mean glare before she trudged off. When she was gone, Debbie Lee opened the door wider. "Come on in, Gracie. You'll have to pardon my sister. Mama and Daddy spoiled all the goodness right out of her. Mix that with her man craziness, and she's a real hot mess." She led Gracie to the dining room where she motioned at the table, which was covered with a Disney princess tablecloth. "Just put those down there and I'll run and get your tip for delivering them."

"There's no need for that," Gracie said as she set the box down. "I was happy to do it."

Debbie Lee smiled. "Winnie is right. You've always been sweet. And just so you know, she's lying to you about Dirk liking spicy women better. According to what she told me, the only thing she got from Dirk was a ride home when she'd drank too much at Becky's wedding."

Gracie couldn't hide her shock. "But she gave him a hickey."

Debbie Lee rolled her eyes. "One I'm sure he didn't ask for."

"Debbie Lee!" Mrs. Crawley yelled. "We need more streamers."

"Be right there, Mama!" Debbie Lee ushered a confused Gracie back to the door.

Gracie continued to feel confused the entire drive out to the ranch. She knew why Winnie had tried to make her jealous. Winnie had never liked her. But she couldn't understand why Dirk had gone along with it. The only plausible answer was that he'd played along with Winnie to discourage Gracie's affections. And the only reason he'd do that is if he didn't hold the same affection. He liked her. He desired her. He might even be a little jealous of other men around her. But he didn't love her. She knew that. She'd always known that. And yet she still didn't want to let him go.

When she arrived at the house and got out of her car, she couldn't help looking at the barn. She should say goodbye. Brandy deserved that. But panic gripped her at just the thought. She turned from the barn and started for the porch when she caught a scent that made her freeze in her tracks.

Burning hay?

With Cole and Emery in Austin, there was no one there but her. She hesitated for only a second before she ran to the barn. Once inside, she immediately saw the pile of burning hay. She grabbed a nearby horse blanket and tried to beat the flames out, but it only seemed to make the fire worse.

"Get back!" Dirk ran into the barn with a hose, and she had never been so happy to see someone in her life. He started spraying down the hay with water. "The horses," he yelled. "You need to get the horses out."

She dropped the blanket and ran to the stalls. She opened each stall, shooing the horses toward the back door of the barn and into the paddock. The only one who didn't come out of her stall was Brandy. Cole had said that the accident had made Brandy skittish. But Gracie hadn't realized to what extent until she stepped into the stall and saw her terrified horse. Brandy was cowered into one corner, her eyes wide and wild.

"Easy, girl." Gracie grabbed a coiled rope from a hook on the wall and slowly moved into the stall. "There's no need to be scared anymore. The accident is behind us. We survived. We're okay."

The words seeped into Gracie's consciousness, and she finally accepted their truth. There was no reason for her to be scared. Certainly not of this horse who loved her. She had survived being thrown. She'd survived losing her father. And even losing her mother. And she was okay.

She was okay.

Tears streamed down her cheeks as the epiphany hit home. She felt like a vise had been removed from her chest and she could breathe again. All her fears and worries about things changing slipped away. No matter what happened in her life, she was strong enough to deal with it.

She clicked her tongue like she used to when she wanted Brandy's attention, and the horse instantly calmed. She stared at Gracie with love and trust in her deep brown eyes.

"That's my girl," Gracie said as she slipped the rope around Brandy's neck. She led the horse out of the stall. When they were safely in the paddock, she slid her arms around the horse and pressed her tear-soaked cheek against her silken throat.

Horses couldn't hug, but it felt like a hug when Brandy used her head to pull Gracie closer. She nickered softly and bounced her head as if to say, "I missed you. I'm glad you're back."

"Oh, Brandy," she whispered in a choked voice, "I'm so sorry. I'm so very, very sorry." The horse pulled away and nudged at Gracie's front jean pocket. A pocket she used to carry the horse's favorite candy in. Obviously, horses didn't dwell in the past. They only lived in the present.

Gracie laughed. "Sorry, girl, but I didn't bring any peppermint candies this time. But I promise I will next time. Right now, I need to help put out a fire."

"The fire's out."

She turned to find Dirk standing not more than a few feet away. His gray eyes were soft with emotion, as was the smile that tipped the corners of his mouth.

"I'm going to assume that I'm not getting a horse."

She took an uneven breath. "I can't let her go."

Dirk gave a brief nod before he took a step closer. And another. And another. Until the toes of his boots were touching the toes of hers. "I know how you feel." He brushed a tear from her cheek with the pad of his thumb. "I'm having the hardest time letting go." He lowered his head and kissed her. It was a mere brush of lips followed by the heated rush of her name. "Gracie."

The single word was spoken with the same longing that was inside of her. At one time, she had longed for him to love her like she loved him. But now she just longed for him to touch her and keep touching her . . . until it was time for him to go.

She drew back, then took his hand and led him through the barn. Dirk had completely drenched the hay with water, and surprisingly, there was only a small amount burnt. When she was battling the fire, it felt like the entire barn was going up in flames.

"Thank you for coming to my rescue," she said as she led him past the hay.

"You probably would've managed without me." He followed her out of the barn. "Where are we going?"

"To my bedroom."

He stopped in the middle of the yard, pulling her short. "No, Gracie. As much as I want to, we can't."

She turned to him. "I'm not that young girl in the wheelchair anymore, Dirk. I don't need protecting or coddling. I'm a woman who can stand on her own two feet and who knows what she wants. And I want this." She pulled him toward the house.

He lagged back, but didn't resist. When they reached her room, he turned her to face him.

"Tell me you've done this before."

She slowly shook her head. "I wanted my first time to be with a man I respect. A kindhearted man who helped me find my smile and gave me hope when I had none."

His expression was almost pained. "Damn you, Gracie. Damn you for making me love you when I'll only break your heart." She barely had time for the words to register before he pulled her into his arms and kissed her. It was a desperate kiss. A kiss that was filled with a bittersweet hunger that took all thoughts from her head except one.

*Dirk loves me. Dirk loves me. Dirk loves me.*

The chant repeated in her head over and over again as he slowly and expertly removed her clothing. Distracted by the delicious heat of his mouth, she barely noticed as each article slipped to the floor. When she was completely naked, he stopped kissing her and stepped back. His gaze slid over her like icing on a warm cupcake.

"My God. You're perfect." He lifted a hand and ever so slowly traced a line of fire along her collarbone and down between her breasts. "So damned perfect." He traced over the swell of one breast and around her hardening nipple before he spread his fingers wide and cradled her in his palm.

Gracie closed her eyes and released the breath she hadn't even known she'd been holding. "Dirk," came out in the puff of air as his thumb strummed over her nipple.

He lowered his head and took her nipple into his mouth. Little electrons of heat raced from his tugging lips to every part of her body, causing her legs to tremble. Before her knees could give out, he swept her up in his arms and carried her to the bed.

He laid her down, then sat on the edge of the bed and pulled off his boots. He removed his clothing much faster than he had removed hers, and she couldn't help rolling to her side and watching as a muscled back was revealed, followed by two pale butt cheeks that made her mouth suddenly dry. It grew even drier when he turned and her eyes landed on the fully erect penis that jutted out from a nest of light brown hair. Her face heated with embarrassment . . . and a hot wealth of desire.

"If you want to stop, Gracie. All you have to do is say so," he said.

She lifted her gaze, and it locked with his as she reached out and touched the silky length of him.

She'd read enough woman's magazines and romance books to know what to do. She caressed the soft, taut skin only once before taking him firmly in hand and pumping from base to tip. His eyes glazed over, and his lips parted on a tortured groan. His reaction brought her slow-burning desire to a boil. He had always had the power to melt her. It was exciting to finally be melting him. She continued to stroke until he grew slick and wet beneath her hand. But when she leaned in to taste him, he stopped her.

"My turn." He eased her back on the bed with a long, sultry kiss, shifting her until her legs dangled off the edge. He pulled back from the kiss, then spread her legs and knelt between them. His hands gripped her knees as his gaze lowered to her hot center that was completely exposed . . . and pulsing with anticipation. He lowered his head, and she felt the rush of his breath a second before his mouth covered her. The wet heat had her hips jerking in response, and his hands slipped beneath her butt and held her steady as his tongue came out to play.

And oh, could it play. It deeply tasted her before it pulled out to gently dance across her clitoris in gliding sweeps and hungry flicks. Intense sensations built until she clawed the bedspread and pleaded for release with huffy sighs. The orgasm burst through her like a shower of popping sparks. She gripped his head with her thighs and cried out.

When her body finally puddled into the mattress, she opened her eyes to find Dirk kneeling between her legs, grinning. "You just said the f-word."

Her eyes widened. "I did not."

"Oh, yes you did." His grin got even bigger. "I just got sweet Gracie Lynn to say the f-word."

While her face filled with heat, he moved up her body until his forearms caged her head and his breath kissed her lips. His eyes were a deep, intense gray as they stared back at her. "And I think I want to make you say it again." He brushed his lips over hers. "And again . . . and again."

Her embarrassment left, and she slid her fingers through his hair and spoke against his lips. "Then make me. Make me be naughty, Dirk."

He growled low in his throat as he deepened the kiss, his tongue thrusting in a rhythm that had her rubbing against the hard length of him. He drew back from the kiss and moved off her. She watched in a sensual haze as he pulled a condom from his wallet, tore it open with his teeth, and then rolled it on. He returned and kissed her again. This kiss softer and sweeter than the ones before, and when he drew back, his eyes held concern.

"I don't want to hurt you."

She cupped his whiskered jaw in her hands and rubbed her thumbs over his bottom lip. "I know. But if I've learned anything in the last year, it's that sometimes you have to go through a little pain to get to the good stuff."

He touched the tip of his nose to hers. "What am I going to do with you, Gracie?"

"How about make love to me?"

"Yes, ma'am." He reached between them, and she felt the hard tip of his penis part her folds and rub back and forth, spreading wet heat. When she was slick and ready, he pushed inside. There was pain, a burning pain that lasted only a moment before it succumbed to the deep pleasure of being filled with Dirk. Once he was completely inside of her, he froze with his head pressed against the side of hers.

"I'm not an expert," she teased. "But for the maximum pleasure, I think you need to move."

She felt his breath rush out against her ear. "Thank God."

But he was still tentative with his thrusts, pulling out before slowly pushing back in. It took her wrapping her legs around his waist and meeting his next thrust to break his control. Once he was seated deep inside, he released a groan and started thrusting hard. She didn't think she could reach orgasm again. But then Dirk reached between them and flicked a thumb over her clitoris, taking her right long with him to the summit.

Gracie didn't say the f-word, but she did say what she'd been wanting to say to him ever since he'd strutted into her life.

"I love you, Dirk Hadley."

*"Hitting the broadside of the barn from ten feet away wasn't something to be proud of. But when Daisy got excited over her achievement and threw her arms around Johnny, he couldn't help congratulating her with a kiss."*

# CHAPTER TWENTY

❦

"THIS IS CRAZY, DIRK. WE should've waited until morning to do this."

Dirk tightened his arms around Gracie and snuggled his face in her neck, speaking against her soft, sweet-scented skin. "You needed to get back in the saddle."

"I hate to point this out, but you forgot the saddle."

He kissed his way to her ear and nibbled the lobe. "I didn't forget. I just thought we'd fit better without one." He rubbed his hard—growing harder by the second—cock against the sweetness of her bottom and was rewarded with a soft moan that made him smile.

Gracie might've been a virgin, but she wasn't a prude. Something she had proven numerous times in the last few hours. They hadn't made love again because he'd only had one condom in his wallet.

But Sweet Gracie Lynn could do some wicked things with her hands and mouth. And so could he.

He slid a hand along the inside of her bare leg and under the tails of his western shirt she'd donned before their excursion to the paddock. She'd also put on a pair of panties, but he easily nudged them to the side before slipping two fingers into her wet heat.

She sucked in a startled breath, then swatted at his hand. "Stop being naughty in front of Brandy."

"Brandy is too happy to care about what we're doing. She's thrilled to have you riding her again and is prancing around this paddock like a show pony."

"She does seem to be happy, doesn't she? As happy as I am." Gracie leaned her head back on his bare shoulder and looked at him. Her eyes were filled with moonlight and something that made Dirk's heart hitch. "Say it again," she whispered.

He shouldn't have said it the first time, and he shouldn't have said it the dozen times after. But he couldn't seem to help himself where Gracie was concerned. "I love you." He brushed a kiss on her forehead. "I love you." He brushed a kiss on her nose. "I love you." He kissed her lips as he slid his fingers deeper.

She moaned into his mouth and her hand came around his neck. He tightened his hold on her waist and worked his fingers in and out while he pressed his thumb to her clit and allowed the horse's gait to set the rhythm.

Feeling her come apart in his arms was one of the most satisfying experiences of his life. It was like holding a firework as it exploded into a beautiful bloom of colors. It shot thought him with consuming heat, branding him with its brilliance. He knew he would never be the same. Ever.

When the last shimmers had died, he eased out of her and adjusted her panties. "I probably better go," he said. "Cole and Emery are due back from Austin soon. And while Cole will be happy to see you riding Brandy, he won't be happy to see a half-naked cowboy riding with you."

She cuddled against him. "Well, riding with half-naked cowboys makes me happy."

Her words made him think about the cowboys she'd be riding with once he was gone. The thought didn't sit well. It didn't sit well at all. But how could he stay and avoid hurting her? Of course, how could he leave and not hurt her—especially after what they had just shared? Either way, Gracie was going to be hurt. The question was which choice would hurt her less?

It was purely selfish that his mind leaned to staying in Bliss and telling her the truth. There was little doubt that she'd be devastated over Lucy giving up her child. And she'd be plenty pissed at Dirk for lying about it all this time. Not to mention the hang-ups she'd have about them being step-cousins. And what about his promise to his grandmother? She would be shoved into the spotlight once the news got out about her being Lucy Arrington's illegitimate child. Could he do that to Granny Bon?

He was definitely stuck between a rock and a hard place. But the only way out was to make a decision. When Gracie lifted his hand and placed a kiss in the center of his palm, he knew he couldn't leave her. And maybe he wasn't giving her enough credit. She was a kindhearted woman. Maybe once he explained things to her, she would understand the reasons for his deception and keeping his grandmother's secret.

If he wanted to make her understand, he needed to take things as slow as he had with Brandy. Although he couldn't take credit for getting her back with her horse. The fire had brought out Gracie's protective nature. Maybe he could bring out the same nature.

"As much as I'm enjoying this ride," he said. "I can't wait to see you ride Brandy solo. My sister Autumn used to barrel race. She wasn't as good as you are, but she won a few first place ribbons."

She turned her head to look at him. "You have a sister?"

"Three, actually. Triplets. Spring, Summer, and Autumn. Their personalities mimic their season names. Spring is vivacious and lighthearted. Summer is intense and hot-tempered. Autumn is mature and mellow. As much as I love them, it was hell living with three older sisters trying to mother me after our mama died."

"Your mother died?" She squeezed his hand and nuzzled her head against his neck. "I'm so sorry."

He'd brought up his mother in hopes that a little sympathy would go a long way in getting her forgiveness for his lies. But Gracie's sincere reaction brought back all the heartache he'd felt after his mother's passing, and he found himself sharing things that he'd never shared with anyone else.

"I was only eight at the time, and when they closed her casket, I felt like all the happiness had been sucked right out of me. I guess you could say I was a mama's boy. But she made it so easy. She was beautiful and funny and charming. No matter how tired she was at night, she always had time to play or read with me. She worked as a checker at the local grocery store and all her customers adored her. She was one of those people who could make you smile just by being in the same room."

Gracie glanced back at him. "Like you."

"I don't know about that. Most people think I'm more like my dad."

She shook her head. "You're nothing like your father."

Dirk could only hope she felt the same way once she found out about his deception. He tightened his thighs and stopped Brandy, then slipped off the horse and reached up for Gracie. She came into his arms as if she belonged there. And he was starting to accept that she did.

"So where's your family now?" she asked as they headed out of the paddock.

"My sisters live in Houston and run their own clothing store. And my grandma lives in Waco in the same house she's lived in since I was born. I think the only way she'll ever leave is feet first. She's one strong-willed woman. But she has a heart of gold."

Gracie waited until he closed the gate before she spoke. "I'd like to meet her one day." There was sorrow in her voice as if it was a wish she knew would never be granted. And since he didn't know if she would ever forgive him for his lies, he didn't know either. After he latched the gate, he pulled her into his arms and held her close, breathing in her innocence.

"I better go and let you get some sleep," he said.

She hesitated for a moment before she spoke. "I've been thinking. It can't be comfortable sleeping on Raff's couch. And there's a queen-sized bed in the apartment over Ms. Marble's garage that is plenty big enough for two."

He drew back with raised eyebrows. "Are you asking me to move in with you, Miss Gracie?"

Even in the dark, he could see the cute blush stain her cheeks, but her gaze was direct when she answered him. "Yes, I'm asking you to move in with me. And don't you dare start that 'Miss' business again. I think we're well past that kind of formality."

He couldn't keep the smile off his face. Nor could he keep from slipping his hands under the tail of her shirt and cupping her sweet butt cheeks in his palms. "Yep, I think we're well past that." He laughed when she swatted him. "I'd love to move in with you, sweetheart, but I don't think Ms. Marble would care too much for that arrangement. The woman is a stickler for what's proper." When Gracie's face fell, he pulled her closer and nuzzled her neck. "But I happen to be extremely good at slipping into places without getting caught. And what she doesn't know won't hurt her."

She flung her arms around his neck and squeezed him tight. "I'll make sure I'm moved in by tomorrow night. I just need Cole to help me take over the last of the boxes in my room."

He drew back. "How about if I come over first thing tomorrow morning and help you with that?"

"I appreciate it, but I don't think all the boxes

will fit in my car—or your car. Eventually, I'm going to get you to take it."

He could probably borrow Raff's truck again to help Gracie move, but he was more than a little sick of borrowing people's vehicles. He wanted to drive his woman around in his own truck.

"I'll figure something out," he said. "For now, I want you to go inside and get some sleep. Something tells me that you're not going to be getting very much sleep in the next few days."

A sexy smile lit her face. "Sleep has always been overrated." She took hold of the lapels of her shirt and pulled them apart in a staccato of opening snaps. "How about a little roll in the hay?"

Just the sight of her full breasts and large nipples made him hotter than a roasted jalapeno, and he pulled her inside the barn. Most of the hay was wet, but thankfully, he found one empty stall with fresh hay and a blanket to lie over it.

With no condoms, he didn't intend to have intercourse. But the best-laid plans are easily broken when you have a warm, willing woman in your arms. During a heavy make-out session, she guided him inside. The feel of her hot, tight sheath took most of his brain cells. When she reached orgasm and clenched around him, he almost didn't pull out in time. Even then, he worried that some of his swimmers had jumped the gun. And it wasn't likely that Gracie was on birth control.

He rolled to his side to ask her when he noticed the edge of an envelope sticking out from the hay. An envelope similar to the ones he'd found before. "Did Lucy have a favorite horse?" he asked.

Gracie slowly opened her eyes and smiled a satisfied smile that warmed his heart. "I don't know if she had a favorite, but she loved horses. She used to ride when she was struggling with a storyline. Why?"

He reached for the envelope. "Because I think we just found another chapter."

As it turned out, the envelope was empty. But Gracie was convinced there had been a chapter in it. While they were searching the barn, they heard a car coming up the road. Dirk sent Gracie back to the house with a quick kiss before he hopped in Raff's truck and hightailed it out of there. He honked at Cole and Emery on his way past and prayed they hadn't notice that he was shirtless.

Once he was away from the Arrington Ranch, his thoughts returned to the possibility of Gracie getting pregnant. The thought should terrify him. After his mother had gotten pregnant by his deadbeat dad at such an early age, Dirk had sworn he would never make the same mistake. But with Gracie, it didn't feel like a mistake. The thought of making babies with her felt right. In fact, it filled him with a giddy kind of joy. He could so easily picture her with a baby snuggled in her arms. Or three.

He grinned as the thought of triplets just like Spring, Summer, and Autumn. But he wouldn't be like his father. He would be there for his kids. He'd be there when they took their first steps, said their first words, and rode their first ponies. He'd be there for Gracie, too. He wanted to spend the rest of his life being there for Gracie. And he wanted his life with her to start now.

He picked up his cellphone from the console to

call Granny Bon. It was late, but his grandmother didn't usually go to sleep until close to midnight. This was confirmed when she answered on the second ring.

"I was just thinking about calling you, Dirky."

Since it was so late, he grew concerned. "Is everything okay? Are the girls all right?"

"They're fine. Summer and Spring are arguing over how to run the store, but they're always fighting over something. It's nothing to be concerned about." She paused. "But what does have me concerned is the visit I had from Holt yesterday."

Dirk was relieved Holt was no longer anywhere near Bliss, but mad that he'd taken his money grubbing to Granny Bon. "I hope you didn't give him any money."

"That's what has me concerned. He didn't ask for money. He just visited for a couple hours, and then left. At first, I thought he was just missing your mama because he asked to look through some of my old photo albums. But now I think he was up to something. That man never missed Dotty a day in his life. Do you think that deadbeat has figured things out?"

Dirk had hoped his father was too stupid to put two and two together, but now that didn't seem likely. "He must've figured out that Mama is somehow connected to the Arringtons. It probably wasn't hard to figure out. She and the triplets look just like Cole."

Granny Bon sighed. "Now that he knows, I'm sure that deadbeat will try to get some money out of it."

"There's little doubt of that. But he won't be able

to if we tell the truth first. Maybe it's time we let the cat out of the bag, Granny Bon. Raff already knows, and if Holt shows up spouting his foolishness, it won't be long before everyone else figures it out."

"But it's not your cat to let out, Dirk Hadley."

It was true, but after what had happened tonight with Gracie, he could no longer go along with his grandmother's wishes. "I'm afraid there's a complication. I met a girl, Granny Bon."

There was silence on the end of the phone before his grandmother spoke. "So Raff was right. You *have* been kissing your cousin."

*"No matter how well Johnny kissed, Daisy was not staying in Tender Heart. She was not going to become like her mother and spend her days with a kid on each hip as she slaved over a hot stove."*

# Chapter Twenty-one

ℭ

GRACIE DIDN'T GET A WINK of sleep. And it had nothing to do with the empty envelope they'd found in the barn, and everything to do with Dirk. It was hard to sleep when you'd just found out that the man of your dreams loved you too. After Dirk left, she lay in bed and went over every word he'd spoken to her and every touch he'd given her. When the pink edge of dawn crept into her room, she couldn't stay in bed for a second longer. She quickly dressed in her riding clothes and headed out to Brandy.

With Dirk snuggled up behind her the night before, she hadn't experienced a moment of fear. This morning, there was a hard punch of panic when she settled into the saddle. She ignored it and walked Brandy down the road that led to the little white chapel. Her muscles tensed when they passed the spot of the accident, and feeling her rider's anxiety, Brandy grew skittish.

Gracie lightened her grip on the reins and pat-ted Brandy's neck. "We're okay." Brandy huffed through her nostrils and bobbed her head as if in agreement. Once they got past the point, Gracie guided the horse toward the open pastures. As soon as they were off the road, Brandy broke into a full gallop.

She gave the horse free rein to run as fast as she wanted, and it seemed that the horse wanted to fly. It felt like flying. It felt like Gracie was glid-ing over the pasture in a low-soaring plane. She leaned forward against Brandy's neck and let the cool morning air caress her cheeks and the scent of fresh-cut hay fill her lungs. Her heart swelled with joy and a feeling of sheer contentment. She was finally back home after a long time away.

She let Brandy run until the horse had worked up a good sweat, then she turned her around and walked back to the ranch. When they were almost to the road, she spied Cole sitting on one of his new mares by a corpse of trees. There was little doubt he'd been watching her and Brandy. The emotion on his face said it all. But he didn't bring up her reconciliation with the horse. Instead, he teased her.

"You're looking a little rusty, Brat."

She took the bait. "You think you can beat me?"

"By a mile." He guided his horse next to Brandy.

Gracie would've loved to race, but something she loved more would soon be arriving at the ranch. "I'll have to take a rain check. Dirk is coming this morning to help me finish moving."

Cole didn't look happy with the news. "I said I'd

help you move."

"You keep putting it off."

His lips pressed into a stern line. "I promised Emery I would keep my mouth shut and let you make your own decisions. But you moving away from the ranch is just plain stupid." She started to speak, but he held up a hand. "I know. After your accident and Daddy's death, I couldn't wait to sell the ranch and leave all my troubles behind. But you made me see the error of my crazy thinking. You made me see that this isn't just a ranch. It's our heritage. Yours and mine."

It was hard to keep the tears from her eyes. While she had doubted her stepfather's love for her, she had never doubted Cole's. He loved her unconditionally. No matter what she'd done in the past or what she would do in the future. She could forge a thousand books and rack up millions in debt, and he'd never stop loving her. She leaned over and kissed his cheek.

"I love you, Cole. But this land is your heritage, not mine. Hef knew it when he willed it to you." She held up a hand like he had done earlier. "It's okay. I'm not hurt by that. Hef loved me in his own way. He just wanted an Arrington to own the land and Lucy's house. And that's exactly how it should be. Your children and your children's children should ranch this land just like your ancestors did."

"They will," Cole said. "But I want my son ranching it right alongside your kids."

"Your son?"

He grinned. "I'd be just as happy with a little girl."

She had been so worried that Cole would be stressed out about the baby. She should've known better. "Congratulations, Daddy. I can't wait to spoil my little niece or nephew rotten."

Cole sent her a pointed look. "You can do that much better if you stay right here on the ranch."

"I can't live with you and Emery forever, Cole. I need my own place."

"A place with horses and land. Not some tiny apartment in town."

After riding Brandy, Gracie couldn't deny his words. She didn't know what she wanted to do with the rest of her life, but she did know that she loved horses and wanted to be around them. "Someday I'll get a ranch of my own. But I don't mind living in town for the time being and working for Ms. Marble. I want to help pay my rehabilitation bills."

He scowled. "There's no need for that. They've all been paid."

"What?"

"Your bills have all been paid—even the hospital bills. It has to be Zane. He swears up and down he didn't do it, but I don't know who else would." He released his breath and ran a hand through his hair. "Damn, I hate taking charity. But with the baby coming, I don't really have a choice."

Gracie was completely stunned. Cole was right. Zane was the only one who had enough money to pay the bills, and she could never thank her cousin enough for his generosity. She would pay him back. She couldn't let him take responsibility for her, but she didn't have to worry about Zane going without because of her. She could pay the loan back when she finally decided what to do with her life.

Talk about all her dreams coming true.

"The last year has certainly been a roller coaster ride, hasn't it?" she said.

"You can say that again. One second, we were plummeting down, and the next, we're on top of the world." He grinned. "I guess that's life."

Gracie couldn't help smiling. "I guess so." She set her heels to Brandy. "Race you back!"

The head start helped, but Cole still ended up beating her to the barn. They were both laughing as they swung down from the saddles. They stopped when they noticed the brand new Chevy truck parked in front of the house.

Cole shook his head. "I guess I shouldn't be worried about Zane paying the hospital bills. He's obviously doing pretty damned good if he can afford to buy a new truck every six months. At least this time he took my advice and got a real truck instead of a Dodge."

But when they finished taking care of the horses and headed inside, it wasn't Zane who sat on the edge of the bathtub holding Emery's hair as she threw up. It was Dirk.

A part of Gracie loved him all the more for the caring concern he was showing Emery. The other part was a little jealous over him touching another woman. But her jealousy evaporated when his gaze locked with hers and love sparkled in his gray eyes.

"Good mornin'." He released Emery's hair and got to his feet. "You're up, Big Daddy." He moved so Cole could take his place. "But I think it's only fair to warn you, your woman had huevos rancheros for breakfast and it's not pretty."

Cole cringed. Her brother had always had a weak

stomach, but Gracie was glad to see him dutifully take a seat on the edge of the tub and take over holding his wife's hair.

Dirk stepped out into the hallway with Gracie and closed the door. When he looked at her, she couldn't help the blush that heated her cheeks. A lot had been said and done the night before to blush about. But she didn't have time to feel too embarrassed before he drew her into his arms and kissed her. It was a hungry kiss, like he hadn't been able to wait a second more to touch her. Relief flooded her. She'd been worried that last night was only a dream. That in the light of day, things would be different—Dirk would be different. But he wasn't. He was the same caring, loving man who'd held her in his arms the night before.

He drew back from the kiss and glanced at the bathroom door before leading her outside to the porch where he kissed her again.

"I missed you," he whispered against her lips.

"I missed you too."

He lifted his head and smiled. Not his usual bright smile. This one was soft. And tender. And melted her heart. "So you went riding this morning. I hope you were solo."

Her cheeks flamed even brighter at the thought of what he'd done to her while they rode double on Brandy. But this time, it was more passion than embarrassment. "I was." She fixed the collar of his western shirt and resisted jerking open all the snaps and snuggling against the warm skin of his chest. "But I'd be happy to ride double with you any-time."

He pulled her close, pressing his face into her

neck and releasing a low growl. "How you tempt me, sweetheart." He drew back, and his smile was gone. "But first we need to talk."

Gracie didn't like the sound of that. It sounded too serious. And she wasn't ready to have a serious conversation about their relationship. Probably because she knew what the outcome would be. Even though Dirk loved her, he'd made no promises about staying in Bliss.

"We don't need to talk, Dirk." She looped her hands around his neck and fingered the silky hair that curled there. "I understand that this isn't forever."

He studied her. "What if it was forever?"

She blinked as her heart rate kicked up a few notches. "What do you mean?"

He brushed a strand of her hair off her forehead. "I'm getting ahead of myself. Before we talk about forever, I need to tell you a little bit about my past."

The word "forever" jumped around in her head like a deliriously joyful puppy, and it took a strong will to get it to sit and behave. Dirk didn't mean what she thought he meant. Forever to him was probably a month tops. Still, a month of Dirk was nothing to sneeze at. She'd take it. She'd take whatever she could get.

"I don't need to hear about your past." She pressed her face to the warm skin above his shirt collar and breathed in his scent. He smelled like blue skies and sun-dried sheets. "I bet Cole and Emery wouldn't even notice if we slipped into the barn for a few minutes."

His hands tightened on her waist, and he groaned. "You need to listen to me, Gracie. I'm not a drifter.

I own a business. In college, a buddy and I developed a job search app that helps people find jobs. It's called Headhunters and it's really taken off in the last couple—" He cut off when she popped open one snap and kissed his chest.

"I'm not surprised. You've certainly had enough jobs to know how to get them. Is that how you could afford the new truck?" A thought struck her, and she pulled back and smiled deviously. "We don't need to go to the barn when we can just go for a drive and try out your big backseat." She took his hand and tried to pull him down the porch steps, but he refused to budge.

"Aren't you even going to ask me why I've been working here in Bliss when I already own a billion-dollar company?"

The word "billion" finally broke through her happy, sexual fog. She froze and slowly turned to him. "You own a billion-dollar company?" He nodded, and a prickle of fear tingled up her spine. "But why would you take odd jobs and hitch rides if you own a company that successful?"

"Because I didn't want you to know who I really was." His grip tightened on her hand as if he was afraid she was going to slip away. It was possible. She suddenly felt like she was dangling over a vast canyon about to slide from his grasp and plummet to her death.

"Who are—?"

She was cut off when a Ford Escort drove into the yard and pulled next to Dirk's truck. A brand-new truck he'd bought with a part of his billion dollars. She was so busy trying to put all the pieces together in some sort of cohesive order that she barely paid attention to the young man who jumped out of the car.

"Are you Cole Arrington?" he asked Dirk.

Before Dirk could answer, the front opened and Cole stepped out. "I'm Cole. What can I do for you?"

The young man held out a legal-sized envelope. "You need to sign for this."

Cole moved down the steps to sign the man's electronic signature pad while Gracie remained on the porch, clinging to Dirk's hand. When the courier got back in his car and left, Cole opened the envelope and pulled out a document. As he read, his expression changed from curious to confused.

"What is it, Cole?" Dirk asked.

Cole's eyes lifted. "It looks like your father is suing me for the ranch."

*"It was just Johnny's luck that he would fall for the one mail-order bride who didn't want to be a bride. She wanted adventure. And if Johnny wanted more kisses, he had no choice but to give it to her."*

# CHAPTER
# TWENTY-TWO

W HEN DIRK ARRIVED AT THE Arrington Ranch that morning, his only plan had been to tell Gracie everything. But fate seemed to be working against him. First, Gracie hadn't been there, then Emery had gotten morning sickness, and now Holt was pulling some kind of craziness.

Dirk released Gracie's hand and moved down the porch steps. "Could I take a look at that?" Cole seemed too stunned to argue.

Dirk only got through the first few lines of the lawsuit before his stomach tightened in anger. "There's been a mistake," he said as he folded the document. "But I'll get this figured out, Cole. I promise." He glanced at Gracie who looked completely stunned. "Don't go anywhere. I'll be back to explain everything."

He drove far enough from the ranch that Cole

and Gracie couldn't hear him yelling at his father and parked by the cluster of trees that surrounded the little white chapel. Holt answered on the first ring. Almost as if he'd been expecting the call.

"Good mornin', son. How are you this fine day?"

Dirk exploded. "What the fuck do you think you're doing!"

There was amusement in Holt's voice, which made Dirk all the angrier. "Granny Bon would wash your mouth out with Irish Spring for using words like that. Of course, sometimes the only way to express your emotions is with a good 'fuck.'"

Dirk gritted his teeth. "Just answer the question. What kind of crazy scheme have you come up with this time? How could you possibly think you could sue Cole Arrington for his ranch?"

The sound of his father inhaling came through the receiver. When he exhaled, Dirk could almost smell the cigarette smoke. "I don't know if I'd refer to it as a scheme. I was never good at school, but I think a scheme involves something devious or illegal."

"That includes just about everything you do."

Holt laughed. "Well, you do have a point there, son. But this time, I'm letting my lawyer do everything by the book. She's not much to look at, but she's smart as a whip and has the nicest set of tits you've ever seen in your life."

"She can't be very smart if she thinks you have a chance in hell of getting Cole's ranch. Let me guess, you're going to say that you were injured while working for Cole just like you did to that company who hired you to load horse feed.

"Now I did injure my back lifting those heavy

bags of feed."

"Not so badly that you couldn't make it to the racetrack the next day and, I'm sure, jump up and down in the bleachers rooting for your favorite horse."

Holt inhaled deeply, then exhaled. "I was in horrible pain. Even before Dilly My Dally lost by a nose. And the small amount of workmen's comp I got didn't nearly cover my physical and mental anguish. But that's neither here nor there. I didn't get injured while working for Cole Arrington." He paused. "Except for the sore jaw my own flesh and blood gave me."

Dirk didn't feel the least bit sorry for hitting his dad. In fact, if he were there, he'd hit him again. "Then what's your angle, Holt?"

"No angle this time. This time, I only want what's rightfully mine." He paused. "Your grandma might be too foolish to fight for it, but I'm not."

"What are you talking about?" But as soon as the words were out, the truth dawned on Dirk. Holt hadn't just figured out that there was a similarity between the Hadleys and the Arringtons. He'd figured out that Granny Bon was Lucy Arrington's illegitimate child.

"How did you figure it out?" he asked.

"It was the eyes. Those Arrington eyes are hard to overlook. Your mama hooked me with those hypnotizing blue eyes." He chuckled. "At first, I thought your old granny had been messing around on grandpa with an Arrington. But when I went to her house to get the scoop, I took a little peek in the lockbox she keeps under her bed and found Bonnie Blue's birth certificate."

Dirk slammed his fist on the steering wheel. "You sonofabitch! You broke into Granny Bon's lockbox?"

"Now, don't be blowing a gasket. As her son-in-law, I have every right to make myself at home."

"Did you also have a right to look through her personal things?" Dirk snapped.

"If those personal things have an effect on my children's well being."

His father's gall was unbelievable. "Your children's well-being? When did you ever give a shit about your children's well-being? You don't even know your daughters, and the only reason you took me in was because you needed someone to cook, clean, pay the bills, and drive you home from the bars when you were too drunk to drive yourself."

"It's called the school of hard knocks, and you should be thanking me for putting you through it. If you had stayed with your sisters and granny, you would've been nothing but a pussy who couldn't tie his own shoes without help. I turned you into a self-sufficient man. You wouldn't be the successful businessman you are without your dear old dad." He took another puff. "And if you'd realized that sooner and been a little more generous, I wouldn't have had to go to such extremes."

"I gave you money."

"A thousand here and a thousand there isn't money. That's pocket change. And what I'll be getting from the Arringtons will be more than just pocket change. My lawyer insisted on starting with Cole's ranch because that was Lucy's house, but I figure every one of the Arringtons owes me something."

"They don't owe you anything," he said. "You have no Arrington blood whatsoever."

"But I was married to an Arrington. I was married to Lucy Arrington's only granddaughter until the day she died, and I'm father to her great-grandchildren. And my lawyer thinks that's more than enough."

Dirk wanted to argue, but he couldn't. His mother had never been smart enough to divorce Holt. And as much as Dirk wished otherwise, Holt was his father. Which meant that there was a chance he could lay claim to the house and land that had once belonged to Lucy. And Dirk couldn't let that happen.

He spoke in a low growl. "How much money do you want? A million? Two?"

There was a long pause before Holt answered. "Let me get this straight. You're going to give me two million dollars to drop the lawsuit?"

"Drop the lawsuit and tell your lawyer and everyone else that it was all one of your scams."

Holt laughed. "Damn, that pretty little Gracie must be one fine piece of ass if you're willing to spend so much to keep her in the dark."

It was a good thing that Holt wasn't there because Dirk had never wanted to beat someone so badly in his life. "Take the deal, Holt. Cole's ranch isn't worth losing two million."

"Sorry, son, but no can do. That crappy ranch might not be worth much, but the final book in that Tender Heart series will be. Much more than a measly two million. And I figure if I win the rights to the ranch, I also win the right to any chapters that were found there—including the one I found last night."

"It was you," Dirk breathed. "You were in the barn last night. You started the fire."

"Purely accidentally. Your sweet thing startled me when she pulled up and I was looking at the chapter."

It appeared that his father was even more evil than Dirk had thought. And Dirk finally realized that there was nothing he could do to change that. The only thing he could do was make sure he never went down his father's crooked road.

"Get ready for the fight of your life, old man," he said before he hung up.

He immediately dialed his lawyers and spent an hour giving them all the facts. Then he called his grandmother. She didn't answer so he left a message to call him. He knew what he needed to do next. He needed to head back to the Arrington Ranch and explain things to Gracie. But there were so many complications now that he didn't know where to start.

A movement had him looking at the pasture to the left of the trees. If he hadn't recognized the horse, he would've recognized the corn-silk blond hair that blew in the wind behind the rider. At first, he thought Gracie was riding to him. But when she veered to the right and disappeared into the copse of trees, he knew where she was going. The same place she always went when she was upset.

By the time he got to the clearing, Brandy was riderless and grazing on the wild grass in the meadow. He patted the horse before heading for the chapel. But Gracie wasn't inside the church.

Instead, he found her in the cemetery.

The gate squeaked when he entered, but she didn't turn around. Nor did she acknowledge him when he moved next to her. She sat cross-legged in front of Lucy's headstone. Obviously, she was upset. She had torn most of the pink petals from the roses that rested on the grave. They were scattered over her lap and the ground. He couldn't blame her. He knew how much she loved Cole and the ranch.

"I'm not going to let my father get the ranch, Gracie," he said.

She remained silent for several long seconds before she finally spoke. Her voice sounded distant and hollow. "Even if it should belong to your family?"

Dirk's breath released. "Who told you?"

She plucked a petal and let it fall from her fingers. "Cole called Zane." She plucked another petal. "And Zane called Mason." She plucked another petal. "And Mason called your father's lawyer and discovered the deep, dark secret." She ripped off the last petal and crushed it in her palm. "Lucy's deep, dark secret."

She laughed, but it came out more like a sob. A sob that cracked Dirk's heart right in two. He reached for her, but his hand stopped in mid-air at her words. "It's hard to believe, you know. It's hard to believe that the two women who affected my life the most were both cold-hearted bitches who could desert their daughters without a backward glance."

"Gracie," he whispered. But she didn't look at him. She opened her palm and looked at the crushed rose petal.

"Or maybe it's not as unbelievable as it is pathetic." Her head bounced. "Yes, that's it. It's pathetic. Pathetic that I allowed women like that to have so much power over me." She squeezed her hand into a fist. "So much power over my thoughts and my actions and my wants and even my desires." She finally looked up at him. And he wished she hadn't. Tear tracks covered her cheeks and her eyes held the glimmer of heartbreaking betrayal. "You're like my mom, did you know that? According to everyone who knew her, she was charming and witty and could make anyone fall in love with her. But once she had that love, it was never enough. Just like my love will never be enough for you, Dirk."

"That's not true, Gracie."

But she went on as if he hadn't even spoken. "Of course, it would've been better if I'd found everything out before I had sex with my cousin."

He clenched his hand that was still reaching for her into a fist and let it drop. "Stop it, Gracie."

"Stop what, Dirk?" She jumped to her feet heedless of the rose petals she crushed beneath her boots. Or maybe she knew exactly what she was doing. She seemed as angry at Lucy as she was at him. "Stop telling the truth?"

"It's not the truth."

Her smile melted. "So what is the truth? Or have you told so many lies that you don't know? Let me help you out with that. The truth is that Lucy Arrington had a child and gave it away. The truth is that her great-grandson came to town and lied his way into the hearts of every man, woman, and child in Bliss."

She swallowed hard and tears trickled down

her cheeks. "At first, I couldn't figure out why a man who owns a billion-dollar company would want my brother's ranch. But then, it dawned on me. You don't want the ranch. You want revenge. Revenge on the Arringtons for what Lucy did to your grandmother. And the best way to get that would be by taking Cole's ranch . . . and by screwing over the Arringtons' Baby Girl."

If she'd had a knife in her hand and rammed it into his chest, it couldn't have hurt more. He tried to remind himself that she was upset. That she didn't mean what she was saying. But it didn't ease the pain of her thinking for even a second that he was capable of that kind of hate and deception. He thought she knew him better then that. But how could she know him when he hadn't been honest with her?

She turned to leave, but he grabbed her arm. "I can explain. If you just listen, I can explain everything." She jerked away as if burned and spoke in a cold voice that chilled him straight to the bone.

"No. I won't be pulled in again. I won't be pulled in by your bright smile and your teasing charm and your words of love. I won't be like poor Hef Arrington who ruined his life because he believed my mother's lies. He believed her when she left him the first time with their young son. He believed her when she left him the second time with her illegitimate kid. And he believed her when she came back the last time and took every cent we'd saved for the horse ranch. I'm not that dumb, Dirk. I'll never sacrifice my family for a liar. Never." She shoved past him and strode out of the cemetery.

*"Daisy woke to the feel of cold, hard steel pressing into her side and a low, whispered voice in her ear. 'Make one sound, pretty lady, and you're dead.'"*

# CHAPTER
# TWENTY-THREE

❧

"AS FAR AS I CAN tell, Holt Hadley doesn't have a case." Mason spoke to the entire room. A room filled with Arringtons. Angry Arringtons. But no one was angrier than Gracie. Her body practically vibrated with the rage she was struggling to suppress.

"Then why the hell did the lawyer take the case?" Cole snapped. He stood at the window looking out at the ranch. A ranch he might soon lose.

"Calm down, Cole," Emery said. "Losing your temper isn't going to fix anything."

"I don't blame Cole." Zane sat on the couch next to Carly. "I'm pissed too. I gave the man a job and this is the thanks I get."

"I feel so bad about recommending him," Carly said. "I just assumed he would be as hardworking and honest as . . ." She let the sentence drift off, but everyone in the room knew who she was talking about. They had yet to bring up Dirk's name. It was like they were too stunned by his betrayal to speak it.

Gracie wasn't stunned anymore. She was livid. She twisted the throw pillow she held in her hands as if it were Dirk's neck. She glanced over to see Becky watching her. She and Mason had arrived back in Bliss soon after Zane had called Mason and the entire family had gathered at the Arrington Ranch to deal with the problem.

*Are you okay?* Becky mouthed the words.

Gracie wasn't okay. She felt like she'd been in a hit and run, and the split second before she'd been flattened to the ground, she'd recognized the driver as a man she'd come to love and trust. She shook her head and twisted the pillow tighter as Mason spoke.

"The only reason Susan Fletcher took the case was because she's a new lawyer and she's looking to get some media exposure out of this."

"What do you mean media exposure?" Carly asked.

Zane fielded his wife's question. "Once word gets out about Lucy's illegitimate child, there will be a media frenzy. This lawyer wants to be right in the middle of it to make a name for herself."

"And unfortunately, the frenzy has already started." Mason pulled out his cellphone and tapped it a few times before handing it to Zane. "This is circulating on Twitter. It's only a matter of time before the news networks get ahold of it and start swarming."

The phone was passed around until Cole got it. He clenched his fist and spoke the name everyone had been avoiding. "I'm going to kill Dirk."

Gracie wanted to second that. If not kill him, then at least ruin his fake, lying smile by knocking out every one of his pearly white teeth. And she wanted to be the first one to take a swing. Or maybe a roundhouse kick would do the job better.

"You don't mean that," Emery said. "You can't hurt Dirk. He's your cousin, Cole."

*Cousin.* Gracie's fingernails dug into the fabric of the pillow. She was trying to forget that she'd had sex with her cousin. Her step-cousin, but that didn't matter. Zane and Raff were step-cousins too, and she'd never considered them as anything but family.

"He's not my fuckin' cousin!" Cole yelled. As soon as the words were out, he apologized. "I'm sorry, but I refuse to accept a man as kin who lied to us for months so he could get his hands on my ranch."

"He isn't trying to get his hands on your ranch," Emery said. "His father's behind the lawsuit, not Dirk."

"Holt Hadley's name might be on it," Zane said, "but Dirk was the one who spent months casing our ranches and businesses before he called his father. He went from Cole's ranch to mine to Carly's diner. I wouldn't be surprised if we all don't receive lawsuits in the next few days."

Mason shook his head. "That doesn't make sense. If Dirk wanted your land and businesses, he would be the one suing. He would stand a much better chance of winning if the birth certificate turns out to be real and he's Lucy Arrington's great-grandson."

"The birth certificate is real."

Everyone turned to Raff, who until this point had been standing quietly by the fireplace. Gracie suddenly realized that he was the only Arrington who didn't look mad. And that was strange. Raff was usually the hothead of the family. The one who lost his cool much worse than Zane and Cole. But he looked calm and collected—if not a little guilty. She soon understood why.

"I'm the one who found the birth certificate in Lucy's hope chest. I'm the one who went looking for her daughter. And I'm the one who brought Dirk here."

It was like she was in a bad horror movie and all the people she trusted were suddenly zombies turning against her. "But why didn't you say anything?" she whispered.

Raff turned to her. "The same reason Dirk didn't tell you. It wasn't our truth to tell. It's Bonnie Blue's. She was the one our family rejected. She should be the one who gets to choose whether to claim us or not. And if anyone should understand that, Gracie, you should. When I left here after your accident I didn't plan to go looking for Lucy's child. I planned to hunt down your mother and tell her about your accident. I thought that if I could convince her to come here and show her only daughter a little love and compassion that it might motivate you to walk again."

It was impossible to keep tears from springing to her eyes because she knew what the outcome of that quest had been. "And she refused."

Raff took a deep breath before he releasing it. "Yes." Cole cussed under his breath and started for

Gracie, but she held up a hand.

"I'm okay, Cole." She turned to Raff. "So why go in search of Lucy's daughter?"

"Because I realized that I was doing the same thing your mother was doing. I was selfishly ignoring a member of our family. I was doing it to protect Lucy and the Arrington name, but that didn't make it right."

Gracie couldn't help wishing he had remained selfish. "So you found her. Why didn't you bring her back yourself?"

"Because she denied being adopted. And I can't blame her. Would you trust a guy who looked like me if I came knocking on your door? But she trusted me enough to send her grandson to check things out." He glanced at Cole. "He didn't come to case your property. He has plenty of money of his own. He was the one who paid Gracie's doctors' bills."

The truth should've made Gracie feel more forgiving of Dirk's lies. Instead, this final deception made her snap. She threw down the pillow and jumped to her feet. "It doesn't matter if he paid my bills! He's still a lying, deceitful snake and I hate him!"

Everyone in the room stared at her as if she'd morphed into someone they didn't recognize. Baby Girl never got angry or shouted or cussed. Baby Girl was sweet and shy and . . . a doormat for any no-good drifter who passed through to wipe his feet on. Well, Gracie was through being a doormat. And she was through being Baby Girl.

"If you'll excuse me." She turned and walked out of the room. She only made it halfway down the hallway before Becky caught up with her.

"Holy crap! I leave town for less than a month and all hell breaks loose." She hooked her arm through Gracie's and none-too-gently tugged her toward her bedroom. Once there, she glanced around at all the boxes. "I thought you were all moved out?"

Gracie d ripped the tape off one of the boxes. "I've changed my mind. I'm not going anywhere. I'm going to stay and help Cole fight for his ranch." She grabbed a barrel-racing trophy out of the box and slammed it down on her dresser.

"Cole is not going to lose the ranch. Didn't you hear Mason? Holt doesn't stand a chance. And from what I could tell, you don't seem to be angry at Holt as much as Dirk. What happened between you two while I was gone?"

"I don't want to talk about it." If she talked about it, she would toss the trophy right through the window. Behind her, Becky released an exasperated sigh before she grabbed Gracie.

It was a known fact that Becky was one of the best cattle wranglers in the state of Texas. She had won just as many trophies and ribbons at steer roping as Gracie had won barrel racing. This was proven by how quickly she had Gracie facedown on the floor with her arm behind her back.

"Oww!" Gracie wiggled. "Let me go, Beck. That hurts."

"It's going to hurt more if you don't spill. What turned my even-tempered friend into . . . me?"

Since Becky never quit until she got what she wanted, Gracie gave in. "Fine! You want to know what happened, I'll tell you what happened. I had sex with him!"

Becky released her arm and rolled her over. "You had sex with Dirk?" She thumped down on her butt next to Gracie. "But what happened to waiting until you were married? What happened to waiting for your Honey Bee?" Her eyes widened. "OMG. Dirk's your Honey Bee."

She sat up. "That jerk could never be my Honey Bee."

Becky studied her before she smiled knowingly. "Oh yes he is. I know you, Gracie Lynn Arrington. And you would never have sex with a man you didn't love."

"Well, I don't love him anymore."

"But does he love you? He must if he paid your doctor bills."

It was hard to talk around the tear-filled lump that formed in her throat. "You don't love someone and lie to them."

"That's not exactly true. I love the daylights out of Mason, but I lied like a cheap rug when I took credit for cooking that spaghetti dinner I ordered after I exploded another potato in the microwave. And I lied when I said I didn't know where his wool suit pants were. I mean how was I supposed to know that if you wash wool it shrinks to a munchkin size?"

"Those are all innocent fibs. You didn't lie about who you were."

Becky rested her arms on her knees. "Dirk is still the same person, Gracie. The only difference is that now he's related to us."

"Exactly! I would've never fallen for him if I'd known he was my cousin."

Becky rolled her eyes. "He's not your cousin. It's not like you and Dirk have the same blood or even grew up in the same family."

"But he should've told me. He should've given me all the facts before I fell in love."

Becky nodded. " When things started getting serious, he should've confided in you. But maybe Raff is right. Maybe it wasn't his secret to tell."

"It was my secret."

Gracie and Becky turned to see Raff standing in the doorway with an older woman. A woman with salt and pepper hair . . . and gray eyes. Gracie knew who she was even before Raff introduced her.

"Becky and Gracie, I'd like you to meet Bonnie Blue . . . Arrington."

The woman's eyes flickered with surprise before she corrected him. "Bonnie Blue Davidson. But just call me Granny Bon. Everyone does."

Gracie was too shocked to do anything but stare, but Becky got to her feet and held out a hand. "I'm Becky. Welcome to the family, Granny Bon. We're not much to look at, but we'll grow on you."

Granny Bon laughed as she took Becky's hand. Her smile was so much like Dirk's that Gracie's breath caught in her chest. "Now that's a bunch of nonsense if ever I heard it. I just got finished meeting the rest of the family and there's not a homely one in the bunch."

Becky squinted. "Are you sure you met my brother Zane?"

Raff chuckled as he reached out and hooked Becky by the arm. "Come on, you hellion. Carly is making dinner for our guest and needs your help." Since everyone in the family knew Becky hated to cook, Gracie figured it was an excuse to leave her alone with Granny Bon. She didn't want to be left alone with Dirk's grandma.

She got to her feet. "I'll help too."

Raff shook his head. "You entertain Granny Bon. Just don't fill her in on all the stunts I've pulled over the years."

Since she couldn't be out-and-out rude, Gracie had no choice but to stay. Once Raff and Becky left, an awkward silence ensued. She could feel Granny Bon studying her. To get away from those probing gray eyes, she quickly pulled out her desk chair. "Would you like to sit down?"

"Thank you." Granny Bon took a seat. She glanced at the boxes. "Are you moving?"

"I was going to move into town, but now I'm not leaving Cole's ranch." She emphasized Cole's and dared Granny Bon to contradict her. The woman didn't.

"It's a beautiful ranch. It looks exactly how Dirk described it." She smoothed out the wrinkles in her floral dress. "I guess you're a little miffed at my grandson. And I can understand why. But you need to know that he wanted to tell the truth. I was the one who kept him from it."

"Why?"

Granny Bon paused for a long moment before she released a sigh. "I guess I was scared. It's tough living with the knowledge that your mama didn't want you. You spend your entire life looking for some explanation for such a cold act, and the only one that makes any real sense is that something is wrong with you. You weren't cute enough. You weren't healthy enough. You weren't good enough."

Gracie didn't reply. She couldn't. Granny Bon was expressing all of Gracie's own insecurities, and all she could do was sit there with a knot in her stomach as the woman continued.

"I told Dirk that the reason I didn't want him telling anyone about me was because I didn't want to intrude on your lives and drag Lucy's name through the mud. But the real reason is that I was scared you weren't going to like me. That I wouldn't measure up to the great Arrington family."

Gracie knew how she felt. She'd felt that way all her life. No matter how well she did in school, or how many ribbons she won at barrel racing, or how many chapters she found of the last Tender Heart book, it would never be enough to make her worthy of the Arrington name. And maybe that was why she hadn't wanted to leave the ranch. Maybe she was afraid that if she did, she'd be easily forgotten.

She swallowed hard. "But you have Arrington blood running through your veins. You don't have to worry about fitting in. You fit already."

Granny Bon's eyes were empathetic and understanding. "Oh sweet child, fitting in has nothing to do with blood. It's about finding people who love you for who you are. My husband Billy was one of those people. He made me realize that I was worthy of love—that my mother leaving me had nothing to do with me and everything to do with her."

Cole had repeatedly told Gracie this, but it hadn't sunk in until now. Her mother deserting her wasn't her fault. As an innocent baby there was nothing Gracie could've done to make her mother love her. Just like there was nothing she could do to make the Arringtons stop loving her. She didn't have to work for love. True love was given freely and with no strings attached.

As if Granny Bon had read her thoughts, she reached out and took Gracie's hand and squeezed it. "From what Dirk tells me, the Arringtons love you, Gracie. You *are* part of their family." She paused before flashing a bright smile. "And I hope I can talk you into becoming part of the Hadleys too."

*"It was pretty dastardly to kidnap a woman like an outlaw. But love made people do crazy things."*

# CHAPTER
# TWENTY-FOUR

❦

THE ENTIRE TOWN OF BLISS, Texas, had gone crazy.

Dirk couldn't walk down the street or eat at the diner without people gawking at him in reverent awe. Like he wasn't the man they'd known for months. Like he was Elvis come back from the dead. The Sanders sisters asked for his autograph. Joanna Daily asked if he'd speak at her book club. Her husband, Emmett, wanted him to pose for a picture he could hang over the cash register at the gas station. And Mrs. Crawley was so thrilled to have him staying at the motor lodge that she gave him a twenty percent discount and the room with the vibrating bed.

Besides the crazy citizens, newspaper reporters had arrived in town in droves and stalked him wherever he went, snapping pictures and asking stupid questions about what it was like to be Lucy's great-grandson.

It was damned annoying. That's what it was like.

He was so annoyed with all the attention that he'd taken to staying in his room and driving out of town for his meals. Not that he felt much like eating. Or sleeping. Or watching television. He mostly just lay on his bed and thought about Gracie.

His emotions vacillated from guilt to anger. When he felt guilty, he recalled every tear he'd made Gracie cry and mentally beat himself up for not telling her who he was as soon as she'd wheeled into the barn that very first day. When he was angry, he focused on the hatefulness of the words she'd yelled at him.

*I'll never sacrifice my family for a liar. Never.*

It was true he had lied, but she hadn't even given him a chance to explain. Instead, she'd assumed the worst. She'd thought he'd actually made love to her out of revenge. It hurt that she could think so little of him. Maybe he'd been right to begin with. Maybe she had never been in love with him. Maybe it was only a crush—an infatuation that crumbled when she realized he wasn't as perfect as she'd thought. Well, she wasn't so perfect either. She had a bad temper. She was unforgiving. And she was a grandma stealer.

The latter really ticked him off.

When Granny Bon called and told him she was in town, he'd immediately felt an overwhelming sense of relief. More than anything, he needed a big grandma hug and some sympathy. He got neither. Instead, his grandmother was all giddy about meeting her new family.

It seemed that Granny Bon had taken to the

Arringtons like a duck to water. And they had taken to her. While he'd been holed up in the motor lodge eating cold pizza and drinking warm beer, she'd been cuddled in Cole's guestroom, reading through the Tender Heart series and looking at family picture albums. When Dirk wanted to come see her, she'd brushed him off like lint on a suit jacket.

"I think it might be best if you waited, Dirky," she'd said. "You aren't exactly popular with the Arringtons right now. But I'm working on getting you back in their good graces."

Dirk should've told his grandmother not to waste her time. If they could so easily turn on him after everything they'd been through together, then he didn't want back in their good graces. He didn't need friends who didn't trust him. Or a family. Or a girlfriend. Not that Gracie had been his girlfriend. She never got a chance to be his girlfriend. They'd gone from friends to lovers to enemies so quickly that Dirk felt like he was suffering from whiplash.

He rolled to his side and glanced at the cowboy clock. It was only ten seventeen in the morning and it already felt like it was ten o'clock at night. He should leave. He should pack up his duffel and head straight out of town. There was no reason for him to stay. The truth about Lucy's illegitimate kid was out, and Granny Bon had been united with her birth family.

And yet, he couldn't seem to get out of bed. Although he got out quickly enough when someone knocked on the door. A woman. He knew a female rap when he heard one. He grabbed a pair of jeans and pulled them on. It was probably Winnie wanting to clean his room, or more likely, snap a picture of Lucy Arrington's grandson for her Instagram.

But what if it wasn't Winnie? What if it was someone else? He quickly slipped on a shirt, and then smoothed down his bedhead. He tried to calmly open the door, but ended up almost jerking it off the hinges in his rush to see who stood on the other side. It wasn't Winnie, but it wasn't whom he'd hoped for either.

"Good morning, Dirk," Ms. Marble said.

He tried to conjure up a smile, but it took too much effort. "Hey, Ms. Marble."

She sent him a censorious look from beneath the brim of her straw bonnet. "Hay is for horses. It's not a proper greeting."

"Yes, ma'am." He cleared his throat. "Good morning, Ms. Marble." She stared him down until he moved out of the doorway and motioned with his hand. "Won't you come in?"

"Thank you." She stepped past him into the room, and he immediately wished he hadn't extended the invitation. The room looked like he felt—trashed. Pizza boxes, fast food containers, and empty beer cans littered the tops of the dresser and nightstand and dirty clothes and towels were scattered everywhere.

He grabbed a pair of dirty boxer briefs off the floor and stuffed them in his back pocket. "Excuse the mess. I wasn't expecting company."

"No need to apologize." She held out a plate that was wrapped in yards of plastic wrap. "I made you some chocolate chip cookies."

It was the first sincere gesture he'd received since the news had gotten out. He should've known that Ms. Marble would be the one person in town who treated him like she always had.

He took the plate and couldn't help bringing her into his chest for a quick hug. "Thank you, Ms. Marble. You're a good-hearted woman, and I'm going to miss you."

She pulled back and straightened her bonnet. "Don't tell me that you're still trying to leave Bliss."

He nodded. "It's time."

"I guess that means you're not going to take your rightful place in the Arrington family."

"I don't belong here." He set the plate on a pizza box, and when he turned, Ms. Marble was pinning him with her steely blue eyes.

"I think we both know that's a lie. You knew you belonged here the second you stepped foot in Bliss. That's why you've stayed so long."

"I stayed so long because I was looking for the truth."

She slowly shook her head as if he was a kindergartener who had gotten the answer wrong. "Your grandmother was looking for the truth. You were looking for a home."

He started to deny it, but then realized he couldn't. Ever since his mother had died, he'd felt like a piece of driftwood bobbing in a vast sea. He loved his Granny Bon's house, but it had never felt like home. Nor had the numerous apartments and trailers he'd lived in with his father. He'd bought a house in Dallas and tried to make it a home. But it was just a decorated shell where he showered and slept. Which was why he did so much traveling.

He thought he'd gotten his restless gene from Holt, but he hadn't been restless as much as searching. Searching for the place he could finally call home. But sadly, the revelation came too late. Bliss couldn't be his home. Not while it was Gracie's.

"I can't stay. Gracie hates me." Each word felt like a knife straight through his heart.

"That girl doesn't hate you. She's upset and I think she has a right to be. You should've told her who you were."

He flopped down on the bed and rested his forearms on his legs, staring at the floor. "I didn't want to hurt her. And the truth did hurt her. You should've seen her at the cemetery sitting by Lucy's grave ripping up those pink roses. It broke her heart to realize that a woman she'd idolized all her life was as cold and unloving as her mother."

Ms. Marble sat down next to him. "But that's not the truth. Lucy wasn't cold and unloving."

He lifted his head to stare at her. "How can you say that? Lucy left my grandmother at an orphanage. At least Gracie's mother left her with a loving family."

There was a long stretch of silence before Ms. Marble spoke. "Lucy didn't leave Bonnie Blue at the orphanage. Lucy wanted to keep her baby. But she was only fifteen with no husband or even a boyfriend. Her parents convinced her that it would be best for everyone if she put the baby up for adoption. They sent her to Dallas to have the baby, and her father promised her he'd found a loving family to adopt Bonnie Blue. When she returned, she wasn't the Lucy I had grown up with. She was despondent and depressed. The only time she was happy was when she was lost in a Tender Heart story. It wasn't until later that she learned her father had lied. He hadn't found a loving family to adopt Bonnie Blue. Instead, he had a ranch hand leave the baby at an orphanage. Lucy tried to contact the orphanage. But by that time, it was too late. Bonnie Blue was already grown and gone and no one knew where. The doctors say that cancer killed Lucy, but I think it was heartbreak. She never forgave herself or her family."

Dirk sat there stunned. Everything made sense now. Lucy never marrying. Her sad look in all the pictures. Her spending all her time writing happily-ever-afters that she would never have. "That's why she didn't leave her family any royalties from her books," he said.

"That's exactly why."

He looked at her. "Why didn't you say anything? Why didn't you tell the Arringtons the truth so that other generations would understand?"

Tears glittered in her aged eyes. "Because I loved Lucy like a sister, and she made me vow to keep her secret."

Dirk knew how hard it was to keep a secret for a few months. Keeping a secret for decades must've been agonizing. He admired Ms. Marble for that. But there was one secret he needed to know. "Did Lucy tell you who Honey Bee was? Did she tell you the name of my great-grandfather?"

She hesitated for only a second before shaking her head. "She never told me who Bonnie Blue's father was."

It was disappointing, but at least Lucy hadn't kept all her secrets. "You need to tell my grandmother and Gracie what you told me," he said. "You need to let them know that Lucy loved Bonnie Blue. That's why she dedicated the last book to her."

Ms. Marble got up from the bed. "It will be my pleasure." She tugged at one of her white gloves. "And you need to talk to Gracie and tell her how much you love her."

"I told her I loved her, and it didn't make a difference."

"Did you try showing her?"

"What do you mean?"

Ms. Marble rolled her eyes. "I swear sometimes men have nothing but cotton between their ears." She put on her stern teacher look. "Gracie doesn't need someone to tell her he loves her. She needs someone to show her. All you've shown her so far is a bunch of lies." He cringed as she continued. "And you can't expect a woman to find out her man lied and then just smile sweetly and forgive you. Gracie needs time to come to terms with everything before you can prove your love."

"That's what my grandma said," he grumbled.

"Smart woman. I look forward to meeting her."

He could see his grandmother being good friends with Ms. Marble. They were both strong-willed, know-it-all women. "How long am I expected to wait for Gracie to come to terms with things?" he asked.

"As long as it takes." Ms. Marble adjusted her hat before walking to the door.

Dirk followed her. "But how will I know she's ready?"

"You'll know. And I suggest you have your grand gesture prepared when that time comes." She stopped at the door and hesitated before cocking an eyebrow at him.

He quickly opened it for her. "About this grand gesture. You wouldn't have any ideas, would you?"

"Not a one," she said as she stepped outside. "This is all on you, Dirk Hadley." She turned and patted his cheek with her gloved hand. "But I have complete faith in you."

*"Daisy should've been madder than a hornet when her kidnapping outlaw pulled off his bandanna. But she couldn't be angry when her heart felt like it was about to burst from happiness. She still wanted adventure. But now she only wanted it with this man. 'Johnny,' she breathed before he kissed her."*

# Chapter Twenty-five

&

IT HAD BEEN SEVEN DAYS, fourteen hours, and twenty-three minutes since Gracie had seen or heard from Dirk. It seemed that he was as good at listening as he was at everything else. He had listened to the hateful words she'd screamed at him in the cemetery and was staying away. He'd made no attempt to see her or call her or even text her.

Gracie was heartbroken.

At first, she thought he'd left town. But then Ms. Marble mentioned he was staying at the motor lodge. Every time Gracie passed the motel, she looked for Dirk's new truck. It was usually there, parked right outside of room number seven. She wondered what he was doing inside the room. Dirk had too much energy to sit still for long. Of course, maybe he wasn't sitting still. Maybe he and Winnie were inside exchanging hickeys. Just the thought made Gracie madder than a hornet.

Except she had no right to be mad. She was the one who had broken it off with Dirk. She was the one who wouldn't let him even explain. After meeting his grandmother and hearing her story, she understood why he had done it. An Arrington had rejected Dirk's grandmother and left her in an orphanage. Granny Bon had earned the right to decide whether or not she wanted to forgive and become a part of the Arrington family.

Gracie had also chosen to forgive. And a visit from Ms. Marble had helped.

It seemed Lucy wasn't as coldhearted as everyone had thought. She had made a mistake by letting her parents talk her into giving away Bonnie Blue. A mistake that had tortured her for the rest of her life. Lucy's situation had made Gracie rethink the reasons her own mother had given her up.

Her mother had shown no signs of regretting her decision, but maybe she didn't regret it because she knew in heart that she'd given Gracie a better home than she ever could. And for that reason, Gracie discovered enough love in her heart to forgive her mom.

She had forgiven Dirk too. She just wished he had trusted her enough to share his secret. His lack of trust had her wondering if he truly loved her. With each passing day, the answer to that question seemed to be a big fat "NO."

A creaking noise had her eye's flashing open. She sat up and glanced around the small apartment above Ms. Marble's garage. Cole had helped her finish moving in a few days earlier. Leaving the ranch had been hard, but it had also been liberating . . . if a little lonely. She helped Ms. Marble during the day, but at night she had so much time on her hands she'd signed up for online college classes and had started writing a new story. This one wasn't about an insecure woman looking for her mother. This one was about a strong, confident woman and her horse.

Although Gracie didn't feel so strong and confident when the creak came again. It sounded like someone was moving up the stairs. Her gaze flashed to the doorknob and the lock she hadn't locked. Before she could jump out of bed and lock it, the doorknob started turning.

She quickly got up and searched for a weapon. The only thing she found was one of the barbells her new therapist Tina had given her. She grabbed the heavy weight just as the door slowly opened and the shadowy form of a cowboy stepped inside.

Her plan was to hide in the shadows and wait until the intruder moved closer to the bed, and then clobber him over the head with the weight and race out the door. Unfortunately, her plan didn't go as she'd hoped.

The man quickly figured out there was no one in the bed and turned to the corner she stood in. The moonlight coming in the window illuminated his face. She didn't recognize the black felt cowboy hat or the red bandanna he had tied around his nose and mouth. But she did recognize the moonlit gray eyes. Her shocked surprise caused her to lose her grip on the weight. It slipped from her hand and dropped to the floor . . . technically on Dirk's foot.

"Sonofabitch!" He grabbed his foot and hopped around.

"I'm sorry," she said. "But what are you doing sneaking into my apartment?"

The bandanna muffled his words, but it sounded like he said, "I'm kidnapping you."

Before she could completely process this, he spun her around and tied her hands behind her back.

"What—"

A folded bandanna tied around her mouth cut off her words. He turned her back around and pushed down his bandanna. His scruff had turned into more of a beard, and there were dark circles under his eyes like he hadn't been sleeping. She couldn't help feeling a little happy about that. She hadn't been sleeping either.

"Did I tie the ropes too tight?" he asked. "Are they hurting you?"

Completely confused, she slowly shook her head. He dipped his knees and scooped her up on his shoulder. She dangled there like a bewildered ragdoll as he carried her out the door.

She should be putting up a fight. He had no right coming to her apartment in the middle of the night, scaring the crap out of her, and taking her hostage. That was crazy. Especially when he'd had plenty of opportunities to talk to her in the light of day and hadn't done so. But crazy or not, she didn't resist. She was too happy to be in his arms again.

On the way down the stairs, he shifted her weight to get a more secure hold. With her nightshirt tangled around her waist, his hand came to rest on the bare skin of her upper thigh. A zing of desire tingled all the way down to her toes, and when he placed her in the passenger's seat of his truck, she just sort of puddled there like ice cream on hot pavement. He had to lean close to fasten her seatbelt, and his gaze locked with hers. For a second she thought he was going to remove the bandanna and kiss her. Instead, he closed the door and jogged around to the driver's side.

He started the truck and cranked up the heater. When he backed the truck out of the driveway, the headlights flashed over the porch. Ms. Marble sat in her rocker in a white nightgown that matched her snowy white hair. She squinted into the light and waved as if it was every day that a woman was abducted from the apartment over her garage.

As they drove through town, she waited for him to explain his midnight shenanigans, but instead he turned on the radio and nervously shuffled through stations. When they reached the turnoff for the Arrington ranches, he took it. Had he kidnapped her just to bring her back to the Arrington Ranch? They drove for a good fifteen minutes before he stopped in a field on the very edge of Cole's land.

He turned off the engine and released his seatbelt, but didn't say a word. He just sat there staring out at the moonlit field. She had about lost her patience when he finally spoke.

"I know you're still mad at me. And you have every right to be. I shouldn't have lied to you. I should've told you the truth no matter what the consequences." He took off his hat and tossed it to the dashboard before running a hand through his hair. Her fingers tingled with the desire to do the same. "I tried listening to Ms. Marble and Granny

Bon. I tried giving you time to get over your anger. But damn it, Gracie Lynn," he thumped the steering wheel with his fist, "just how long is it going to take for you to forgive me?"

His angry words made her smile against the bandanna. She'd thought he didn't care enough to contact her, and all along he'd been waiting for her to make the first move. And from the looks of things, not too patiently.

"I should've never listened to those two meddling women," he continued. "I certainly shouldn't have listened to Ms. Marble. A grand gesture." He released his breath in a snorted huff. "Although she was probably thinking more of red roses and a fancy restaurant. Instead, I had to go with the crazy stunt I thought up when I was sleep deprived and desperate."

She knew she should feel a little sympathy for him, but she was eating this up with a spoon.

He shook his head. "I just thought that since you love Tender Heart and Daisy McNeil so much that you would think it was romantic. Now it just seems stupid as hell."

*Tender Heart and Daisy?* What did they have to do with Dirk coming to her apartment and abducting—? She froze as the truth smacked her between the eyes. Dirk wasn't acting crazy at all. He was playing out the scene from Gracie's favorite book. And if she hadn't been so happy to see him, she would've realized it much sooner. He had reenacted it perfectly, from the sneaking into her room in the middle of the night to the sexy black hat and outlaw bandanna.

Since there were no words to describe the feeling

of love that burst over her, she slipped her hands free of the loosely tied ropes, unbuckled her seatbelt, and crawled right into Dirk's lap.

He looked surprised for only a second before he flashed a smile. "I guess I'm not too good at tying ropes."

She slipped the bandanna off her mouth before she took his face in her hands. "Something you'll have to work on," she whispered right before she kissed him.

As far as Gracie was concerned, it was the best kiss in the history of kisses. At the first touch, their lips felt like two halves of a whole coming back together after being separated for too long. The kiss was filled with all the emotions they couldn't find words for. When they finally drew back, they were both smiling.

She rested her forehead on his. "You read Tender Heart."

His fingers drew delicious circles on her thighs that straddled him. "I only planned on reading Daisy's story. But my great-grandmother writes better than I thought she did. Once I got started, I couldn't stop until I'd finished all of them."

"Is that what you've been doing in your room for the last couple weeks?"

He stopped caressing her thighs and pulled back. "How did you know I was in my room?"

"Umm . . . Mrs. Crawley mentioned it." She blushed, and he immediately knew.

"Liar." He Eskimo kissed her.

"Look who's talking."

The smile faded, and his hands came up to cradle her face. "I lied about a lot of things, and I apologize for that. But there's one thing I didn't lie about. I love you, Gracie Lynn Arrington. I've loved you since the moment I laid eyes on you. You might've fallen out of your wheelchair, but I was the one who took the tumble."

His thumb caressed her bottom lip. "I tried to pretend that we were just friends, but the first brush of your lips made me realize my mistake. I want you. I want to touch you." His thumb pressed into her lips. "I want to kiss you." He leaned in and gave her a heated kiss. "And I want to lose myself inside you until I'm never found." He pressed the hard ridge of his fly against her panties.

She wanted that too. But as she looked into his beloved eyes, she couldn't help feeling a little scared. "But I don't know who you are," she whispered.

He held her chin as he met her gaze. "You know me, Gracie. I'm the same man who brought you chickens. The one who taught you how to make scrambled eggs. The one who carried you in my arms at Becky's wedding, kissed you in your bedroom, and made love to you in the hay."

He smiled that beautiful smile that had always melted her heart, and always would. "And I'm the man who's going to marry you in a little white chapel and build you the best house Texas has ever seen."

Just like that, all her fear was gone. He was right. She knew him. She had always known him.

"Oh, Dirk!" She hugged him tight before covering his face with kisses.

He laughed. "Aren't you going to ask me where this house is gonna be?"

She stopped kissing him and looped her arms around his neck. "I don't care as long as you're there with me."

She expected him to take full advantage of the fact that only a thin pair of panties and a zipper separated them from nirvana, but instead he opened the door of the truck and slid out. He carried her into the middle of the field.

"I'm thinking we'll put the house right here." He shifted her so he could point. "And the barn over there."

She stared at him. "Here? But this is Cole's land."

He smiled. "Not anymore. We finished signing the paperwork this morning."

Her eyes widened. "You took my brother's land?"

His smile got even bigger. "Now don't go losing that hot temper of yours. I'm not taking his land. And my father's not going to take it either. Once Mason made him realize that he didn't have a chance of getting his hands on the ranch, Holt took the deal I offered him—with the stipulation that he stay the hell away from me and my family and hands over the chapter of the Tender Heart novel he stole from Cole's barn."

Gracie was still confused. "But I don't understand. You're building a house for me on Cole's land?"

"Our land. I bought it from your brother after convincing him that it was the smart thing to do. He doesn't need all this land for his horse ranch, and the money I paid him will cover his new stables. Not to mention that then his little sister will never have to leave her home again." His face grew serious. "This is where you belong, Gracie. This has always been where you belong."

Tears welled in her eyes as a bubble of happiness expanded inside her and filled her to bursting. She hugged him closer.

"No, this is where I belonged, Dirk. Right here in your arms."

*"Johnny was getting married."*

# Chapter
# Twenty-six

☾

"HERE, DRINK THIS. IT WILL help calm your nerves."

Dirk stopped tying his bow tie and lifted an eyebrow at the bottle of tequila his sister, Spring, held out. "Where did you get that?"

"I swiped it from Zane's study."

"For the love of Pete." Summer threw her bouquet of wildflowers at Spring. Having been a softball player, she had great aim. The flowers hit Spring's butt dead center and bounced to the floor. "We don't steal from family."

"Oww!" Spring grabbed her butt and glared. "You can't steal from family. What's theirs is yours. And what's yours is theirs."

"Which explains why you keep borrowing my clothes and forgetting to give them back."

"Be quiet, you two." Autumn walked over and took the bow tie from Dirk's hands. "Dirk doesn't need a catfight on his big day." She studied him closely as she expertly tied his tie. "You're sure this is what you want? It just seems like you're rushing into things. I didn't even know you had a girlfriend until you called me and told me you were getting married."

Since he had sprung the news on his sisters unexpectedly, he couldn't blame Autumn for her concern. She was a person who studied things from all different angles before she made a decision. He waited for her to finish straightening his tie before he pulled her into his arms and gave her a hug. "I've never been more sure of anything in my life." He drew back. "Now stop worrying."

She smiled. "Gracie is lovely. I couldn't have picked a better sister-in-law."

"She is nice," Spring said. "If a little shy."

Dirk had thought that once himself. Not anymore. His shy Gracie had turned into a strong, determined woman who knew exactly what she wanted—in and out of bed. He glanced in the mirror to make sure the collar of his tuxedo shirt still covered the hickey on his neck. He smiled at the memory of her pulling back after she gave it to him. "From this point on, Mr. Hadley, I'm the only one who gets to brand you."

Yep, he was marrying a possessive hellcat. And he couldn't be happier.

The door of Zane's guestroom opened, and Zane stuck his head in. "Okay, Mother Hens, it's time to get to the chapel and do your bridesmaids thing while the men take over."

Autumn and Spring quickly kissed Dirk on either cheek before heading out the door. Summer took her good sweet time following.

"The Arringtons are certainly an arrogant lot."

She picked up her bouquet and stuffed it under her arm like a softball mitt.

"That we are." Zane held the door for her. "And something tells me you have the same family trait."

"As if," she grumbled, but a smile tickled the corners of her mouth as she leaned in to give Dirk a kiss on the cheek. "Try not to mumble the words like you did when you were baptized."

Dirk laughed. "I'll do my best."

After the girls left, his male cousins filed in. While they all had seemed to forgive him for his deception, there was a piece of him that was waiting for the hammer to fall. Or the Arrington fist to fly. It seemed that today might be that day when Raff closed the door and all three cousins circled around the mirror he stood at.

He turned and held up a hand. "I realize there are some hard feelings, but I'd appreciate it if you'd wait to give me my just deserts until after the wedding . . . and honeymoon." He would need all his strength to keep up with Gracie.

The cousins exchanged glances, and Cole shook his head. "I'm afraid we can't do that."

Well, shit. It looked like Gracie's hickey wasn't the only bruise he was going to take to the chapel.

He nodded. "Okay. Let's get this over with." Raff took a step closer, and Dirk braced. But instead of punching him, Raff pulled a small box out of his tuxedo pocket and handed it to Dirk.

Dirk couldn't hide his surprise. Or his relief. "You got me a gift?"

"Sorta," Zane said. "It's more like a . . . hell, I don't know what you would call it. Just open it."

Since it was too small to be a bomb, Dirk didn't

hesitate to lift the lid of the box. He stared in stunned awe at the arrowhead that rested on a wad of tissue paper.

"You probably should've found your own like we had to," Cole said. "But with selling your house in Dallas, starting to build your house here, and your business, we figured you didn't have time to worry about an arrowhead."

Dirk had been pretty busy the last two months. Just not with houses or his company. His realtor had taken care of the sale of the house in Dallas and Dirk had hired an architect and contractor to start Gracie's house. He had also decided to sell his shares of Headhunter to Ryker. Ryker still enjoyed the business while it had lost its appeal for Dirk months ago. He wasn't sure what he wanted to do with the money he made from the sale, but he would figure something out. For now, he just wanted to spend time with Gracie. She was the one who had been keeping him busy, but he didn't think her brother and cousins needed to know that. Especially when he was holding the best wedding gift he could've asked for.

He stared down at the arrowhead, and emotion settled in his throat. He had to swallow twice before he could speak. "Thank you. This means a lot to me."

Zane nodded. "Raff was the one who finally found it. I polished it. And Cole drilled the hole for when you figure out how you want to wear it." He glanced at Cole and Raff. "And there's another gift that goes with the arrowhead. We each want you to have twenty acres of our land."

Dirk shook his head. "You don't need to do that.

Cole already gave me a deal on the land for the house."

"We want you to have it." Raff said. "And it's not just for you. It's for Granny Bon and your sisters if they should ever want to live here. This is your home." He held up his wrist with the arrowhead dangling off the leather lace. "Arringtons . . . straight and true."

Zane followed his lead and pulled the chain from the collar of his tux shirt. Cole pulled out his keychain. With emotion burning the back of his eyes, Dirk picked up his arrowhead and held it tightly in the palm of his hand.

He *was* home.

☾

The wedding was like all the other Arrington weddings. The little white chapel was decorated in flowers and fluff. The pews were packed with family and friends. And the bridesmaids were pretty as October peaches in their apricot gowns. But there was one difference from the other weddings. The bride who walked down the aisle toward Dirk was the most breathtakingly beautiful woman he'd ever seen.

Gracie was dressed in a pure white gown that hugged the curves of her body and flared out around her legs. With her corn silk blond hair, she looked like an angel floating toward him. Her body had gotten stronger, no doubt from all the horseback riding she'd been doing. He figured there would be plenty of first place barrel racing ribbons to come. She still helped out Ms. Marble with baking and had helped bake their wedding cake. And she was also writing a story about a woman and her horse. He had little doubt there would be a happy ending.

"Take care of my brat," Cole said as he handed Gracie off to Dirk.

Dirk couldn't take his eyes off the turquoise blue pools that reflected his love right back at him. "Every second of every day," he whispered before he kissed Gracie's hand and turned to the pastor.

It was a short ceremony, but the reception that was held in Cole's new stables and barn lasted way too long. After they'd cut Ms. Marble's cake and made the toasts, he was ready to take his bride to the hotel suite he'd reserved in Austin, but Gracie was having so much fun dancing that he couldn't ask her to leave. So they danced. They danced long after all of the guests had left. After Cole and Emery had gone to bed. After the D.J. packed up. They didn't need music. They danced to a song only they could hear.

Gracie smiled as they swayed on the wooden dance floor beneath the autumn stars. "It was a perfect wedding, wasn't it?"

He held her close and nuzzled her neck. "Perfect." She giggled when he touched a ticklish spot behind her ear and missed a step. "Are you drunk, Mrs. Hadley?" he teased.

"On love." She sighed with contentment. "I didn't have a drop of alcohol."

He nibbled her ear. "Liar. We toasted with champagne."

"You toasted with champagne. I toasted with ginger ale."

"But why would you—?" He stopped and drew

back, his gaze running over her body. "You're pregnant? But I thought you didn't conceive that night in the barn."

Her cheeks blushed a pretty pink. "I didn't. I conceived the weekend we camped by Whispering Falls." She hesitated. "Are you okay with that?"

"Okay?" He lifted her off her feet and spun her around. "I'm delirious. Ecstatic. Completely overjoyed. I want your babies, Gracie Lynn. Lots and lots of your babies."

She tipped back her head and laughed. "Our babies." When he finally set her on her feet, he noticed the tears glistening in her eyes.

He cupped her chin. "What's wrong, Gracie?"

"I wish they could be here to see our babies."

"Our mamas?"

She nodded. "Although my mama didn't want to be a mother. I doubt that she'll want to be a grandma. I was talking more about your mother . . . and Lucy. I know both of them would've been wonderful grandmothers."

It made him happy that she'd forgiven Lucy and was back to being his great-grandmother's number one fan. "I wish they were here too." He glanced up at the stars. "And maybe they are. I've always felt like my mama watched over me, and Emery is convinced that Lucy has been guiding us to the chapters of her last book."

"I think so too. I think she'll continue until all the chapters are found." She brushed a kiss over his lips. "And all the Arringtons have found their happily-ever-afters."

Dirk had never believed in ghosts or fairytales. He did now. He turned her so her back rested against him and slipped his hands over her stomach. "I was thinking. What do you think of the name Dorothy Lucille?"

"It's a beautiful name, but Emery has already chosen Lucille as the middle name if she and Cole have a daughter."

"So? This is Arrington land. There should be lots of little Lucys running around."

She smiled up at him. "And maybe a Johnny and Daisy."

"Hell yeah. And every other hero and heroine in the series."

Her eyes widened. "That's twenty-two kids. Twenty-three if we name one after Lucy. And I'm not having twenty-three kids."

"Okay. I'll settle for a baker's dozen."

"No."

"Ten?"

"Nope."

"Eight?"

"I'll think about six."

"Deal!"

She whirled around in his arms. "Did you just play me, Dirk Hadley?"

"I sure did, Miss Gracie." With that, he scooped her up in his arms and carried her off into their happily-ever-after.

Here's a sneak peek at the next book in
Katie Lane's
**TENDER HEART TEXAS**
series!

☾

**FALLING FOR A
CHRISTMAS COWBOY**
*is out November 2017!*

# Chapter One

☾

THE NORTHERNER THAT SWEPT IN from the plains two weeks before Christmas didn't bring snow. It brought something worse.

In his travels, Raff Arrington had driven in Minnesota blizzards, Washington rainstorms, Arizona heat, and even a Louisiana hurricane. But damned if this Texas ice storm didn't beat them all. The highway outside of Bliss was slicker than an Olympic bobsledding run and sleet flew from the night skies like incoming artillery fire. Raff was creeping along at thirty miles per hour, and the backend of his '67 Chevy pickup still fishtailed around every curve.

He hadn't planned on stopping in Bliss. He liked to be as far away from his hometown as he could get during holidays. But the weather had caught him by surprise on his way from Houston. Now it looked like he'd have to postpone the delivery he planned to make in Oklahoma.

He glanced over at the 1873 Winchester rifle lying next to him on the bench seat. It was referred to as "The gun that won the west." But in this case, it was more like the "The gun that tamed Texas." He'd been looking for this particular gun for the last two years. And there was a moment when he'd held the smooth wooden stock and cold steel barrel in his hands that he'd thought about keeping the gun for himself. But then he remembered his golden rule.

Never get attached to anything.

He'd bought the gun as a gift. A gift that would hopefully ease the guilt that had been with him since the fire. But it looked like he'd have to deal with the guilt for another day. Ice had started to accumulate on the windshield so quickly it looked like the inside of a snow cone machine. Luckily, he was only a quarter of a mile away from the turnoff to his ranch. Not that his acreage was still a ranch.

At one time, the Arrington Ranch had been the biggest ranch in Texas, but then his father and two uncles had a dispute on the how the ranch should be run—or Cole and Zane's fathers had a dispute. Raff's father, Vern Arrington, was the easy-going middle son who didn't fight for anything. Even things he should fight for. When the other two brothers had decided to split the ranch three ways, Vern had been stuck with the land least suitable for ranching and his great-great-great-grandfather's old rundown cabin. His father had been quite pleased with the cabin and land and had named the ranch after the famous Tender Heart book series that was written by his Aunt Lucy.

Lucy Arrington wrote the series in the 1960's and based it on the mail-order brides brought to Texas to marry the cowboys who ran the Arrington Ranch. As a kid, Raff had loved the series. He stopped loving it when he grew up and realized that happily-ever-afters were purely fictional.

Once he turned off the highway and onto the road to the Tender Heart Ranch, he relaxed and switched the radio from the weather station to country oldies. Loretta Lynn was singing *Country Christmas*. Raff loved Loretta and remembered the song from one of the many Christmas albums his grandmother had played during the family holidays. He could sing about as good as he could ranch and write, but that didn't stop him from belting out the words he remembered. He cut off in mid-verse when a flash of red caught his attention.

At first, he thought it was one of his cousin Becky's Hereford cows running across the road. Too late, he realized it wasn't a cow but a woman in a red dress. And she wasn't running, she was standing right smack dab in the middle of the road.

"Shit!" He slammed on the brakes. The mud wasn't as slick as icy asphalt, but it was slick enough to cause the tires to skid straight toward the wide-eyed woman who was frozen in place. Raff cranked the steering wheel to the right, and the truck slid up a bank and straight into a wooden fence post.

If he had been in a new truck with airbags and a locking shoulder strap, he would've survived the accident without a scratch. But his vintage truck didn't have those amenities. It had a lap seatbelt that kept him in the seat, but didn't keep his head from flying forward and smacking the steering wheel.

For a moment, he saw stars.

Then he saw nothing.

When he came too, it took him a moment to get oriented. His head hurt. His body was being jostled around. And he could smell chocolate . . . and wet animal?

He slowly opened his eyes. Two fuzzy red mountains greeted him. He blinked. No, not mountains. Boobs. A set of big boobs in red knit that showed off every luscious curve. Some guys liked legs. Some guys like asses. But Raff had always been a boob man. He was just thinking about burying his entire face between those lush melons of delights when his fantasy was interrupted by the woman's hysterical voice. A voice that was sweet as southern tupelo honey and extremely familiar.

"Sweet Baby Jesus! Everything has just gone to heck in a handcart. First, Miles runs out on my beautiful August wedding, ruining my plans to become a perfect southern wife and mother. Then my interior design business almost goes bankrupt, ruining my plan to be a successful, independent woman. And when I finally come up with a plan to fix both problems, I end up stranded on a muddy country road in a freezing snowstorm that completely ruins my cashmere sweater dress and Valentino leather shoes. And if that isn't enough to make a grown woman cry buckets, I'm now responsible for keeping a jerk of a cowboy alive." Her breasts rose and fell in an exasperated huff. "If

I didn't know better, Lord, I'd think you were out to get me."

She tried to shift gears, and the loud grinding noise finally had Raff sitting up. Pain ricocheted through his head like a pinball, but it was the needling pain knifing through his balls that got his attention. He glanced down to see a soaking wet cat using his lap as a springboard.

"What the hell!" He shoved the fur ball to the floor. It yowled as the truck swerved to the side of the road and barely missed hitting another fence post before it slammed to a stop. Raff grabbed onto the dash and put an arm out to keep the woman from suffering the same fate that he had. Soft breasts pushed into his forearm as he turned to her.

In the light from dash, she looked like the victim of a drowning. Her wet hair was darker than the usual vibrant red and plastered to her head like a skullcap. Mascara ringed her big blue eyes. And freckles, that he didn't know she had, peppered her pert little nose and high cheekbones. The only makeup that had survived the storm was her lipstick. Her lips looked like they always did. Like an early summer strawberry that had been smashed just enough to spread out the corners but leave the center all plump and juicy.

"Savannah," he said. The word came out sounding like a death toll.

If you enjoyed *Falling for a Cowboy's Smile*, be sure to check out the other books in Katie Lane's Tender Heart Texas Series!

*Falling for Tender Heart*
*Falling Head Over Boots*
*Falling for a Texas Hellion*
*Falling for a Cowboy's Smile*

And coming in November . . .
*Falling for a Christmas Cowboy*

## Other series by Katie Lane

### Deep in the Heart of Texas:

*Going Cowboy Crazy*
*Make Mine a Bad Boy*
*Catch Me a Cowboy*
*Trouble in Texas*
*Flirting with Texas*
*A Match Made in Texas*
*The Last Cowboy in Texas*
*My Big Fat Texas Wedding (novella)*

### Overnight Billionaires:

*A Billionaire Between the Sheets*
*A Billionaire After Dark*
*Waking up with a Billionaire*

**Hunk for the Holidays:**

*Hunk for the Holidays*
*Ring in the Holidays*
*Unwrapped*

**Anthologies:**

*Small Town Christmas*
*(Jill Shalvis, Hope Ramsay, Katie Lane)*

*All I Want for Christmas is a Cowboy*
*(Jennifer Ryan, Emma Cane, Katie Lane)*

D EAR READER,
    Thank you so much for reading *Falling for a Cowboy's Smile*. I hope you enjoyed Dirk and Gracie's story as much as I enjoyed writing it. If you did, please help other readers find this book by telling a friend or writing a review. Your support is greatly appreciated!

    Love,

*Katie*

# ABOUT THE AUTHOR

Katie Lane is a *USA Today* Bestselling author of the *Deep in the Heart of Texas*, *Hunk for the Holidays*, *Overnight Billionaires*, and *Tender Heart Texas* series. She lives in Albuquerque, New Mexico, with her cute cairn terrier Roo and her even cuter husband Jimmy.

For more info about her writing life or just to chat, check out Katie on:
Facebook: *www.facebook.com/katielaneauthor*
Twitter: *www.twitter.com/katielanebook*
Instagram: *www.instagram.com/katielanebooks*

And for upcoming releases and great giveaways, be sure to sign up for her mailing list at
*www.katielanebooks.com*

Made in the USA
San Bernardino, CA
26 January 2019